What the critics are saying...

5 Hearts! "I loved this book. The sex is intense!" ~ *TRS Blue The Romance Studio*

"Turn up the air conditioner, get out the asbestos gloves and get ready to burn when you read *The Abduction of Emma*. Luke and Emma simply sizzle. *The Abduction of Emma* teases, tantalizes, and titillates and will have readers begging for more." ~ *Romance Reviews Today*

"This story heats up at the very beginning and burns hot and sweaty through the whole book. So get out the toys, ice water, and tie down the significant other and enjoy this of love winning once again." ~ *Just Erotic Romance Reviews*

"*The Abduction of Emma* is Ms. Havlir's debut novel with Ellora's Cave, and a dramatic entrance it is! Luke and Emma's relationship is handled masterfully, from the first meeting to the final decision" ~ *Road to Romance*

"*Beverly Havlir* combines erotic passion with loving emotion and creates a genuine love story." ~ *Romance Junkies*

"*The Abduction of Emma* touches on the sexual desires between two compatible and destined people." ~ *Sizzling Romances*

"*The Abduction of Emma* is, without a doubt, a very steamy, erotic, sexy read." ~ *Fallen Angel Reviews*

Recommended Read "*Taming Alex* is hot, sexy and so very fulfilling. I loved every moment of it. Ethan and Alex sizzle with intensity, passion and heart." ~ *Road to Romance*

"*Taming Alex* is a wonderful story about two people who try to fight their intense attraction for each other and wind up falling in love." ~ *Just Erotic Romance Reviews*

"*Taming Alex* is a well-written quickie and one that I highly recommend." ~ *Romance Reviews Today*

"*Beverly Havlir* delivers a powerhouse of a short story. Erotic and loaded with emotion." ~ *Enchanted in Romance*

5 Hearts! "*Taming Alex* is the sequel to *Ms. Havlir's* The Abduction of Emma and proves to pack the same amount of intense emotion and hot sex as her first!" ~ *The Romance Studio*

Beverly Havlir

Insatiable

ELLORA'S CAVE
ROMANTICA PUBLISHING

An Ellora's Cave Romantica Publication

www.ellorascave.com

Insatiable

ISBN # 1419953354
ALL RIGHTS RESERVED.
The Abduction of Emma Copyright © 2004 Beverly Havlir
Taming Alex Copyright © 2004 Beverly Havlir
Edited by Heather Osborn
Cover art by Syneca

Electronic book Publication July 2005
Trade paperback Publication March 2006

Excerpt from *Bodyguard* Copyright © 2005 Beverly Havlir
Excerpt from *Pleasure Planet* Copyright © 2005 Claire Thompson, Beverly Havlir

With the exception of quotes used in reviews, this book may not be reproduced or used in whole or in part by any means existing without written permission from the publisher, Ellora's Cave Publishing, Inc.® 1056 Home Avenue, Akron OH 44310-3502.

This book is a work of fiction and any resemblance to persons, living or dead, or places, events or locales is purely coincidental. The characters are productions of the authors' imagination and used fictitiously.

Warning:

The following material contains graphic sexual content meant for mature readers. *Insatiable* has been rated *E-rotic* by a minimum of three independent reviewers.

Ellora's Cave Publishing offers three levels of Romantica™ reading entertainment: S (S-ensuous), E (E-rotic), and X (X-treme).

S-*ensuous* love scenes are explicit and leave nothing to the imagination.

E-*rotic* love scenes are explicit, leave nothing to the imagination, and are high in volume per the overall word count. In addition, some E-rated titles might contain fantasy material that some readers find objectionable, such as bondage, submission, same sex encounters, forced seductions, etc. E-rated titles are the most graphic titles we carry; it is common, for instance, for an author to use words such as "fucking", "cock", "pussy", etc., within their work of literature.

X-*treme* titles differ from E-rated titles only in plot premise and storyline execution. Unlike E-rated titles, stories designated with the letter X tend to contain controversial subject matter not for the faint of heart.

Dedication

To Jim, my real life hero

About the Author

&

A lifelong reader of romance, Beverly realized that traditional romance books lacked extra "oomph" or spice, to make them truly exciting reads. So, putting pen to paper, or in this case fingers to the keyboard, she set about writing Romantica. Now she's completely hooked.

Juggling writing with a husband and two active kids, Beverly always finds the time to bring her characters to life. A vivid imagination helps, as well as being a true romantic at heart. Her characters inhabit her head, talk to her and make their personalities known. She is more than happy to let them take her where they lead.

Beverly welcomes mail from readers. You can write to her c/o Ellora's Cave Publishing at 1056 Home Avenue, Akron OH 44310-3502.

Also by Beverly Havlir

&

Bodyguard
Jed's Revenge
Pleasure Planet

Contents

The Abduction of Emma

~11~

Taming Alex

~135~

The Abduction of Emma

ఐ

Prologue

※

Luke Forrester stared at the beautiful, smiling image in the framed photograph sitting on his desk. Deep blue eyes, almost indigo, looked directly into the camera. Creamy skin—smooth as silk to the touch—and full pouty lips were parted in a mysterious smile. He clenched his fist and crushed the sheaf of papers in his hand. If what the private investigator's report said was true, Emma Fairchild had just accepted an engagement ring from the man she'd been dating for the past three months. His lips curled in disgust. Michael Rutherford came from a long line of blue-blooded bankers, whose ancestors no doubt came over on the fucking Mayflower. While he...

He had been born and raised on the wrong side of the tracks.

The Fairchilds and Rutherfords moved in the same social circles. Though he now belonged to the same elite group since he'd made his millions, he still felt like an outsider, like he wasn't good enough.

For one thing, he didn't have a pedigreed background like all of them. While their mothers had been in fashion shows and charity balls, his was working three jobs just to keep food on the table.

Luke shifted and sighed heavily. Society was going to go crazy over this prospective union. Even in these modern times, old money inevitably married old money.

But she's mine.

Anger washed over him, anger he had felt since reading the report he had received. Emma Fairchild was, and always would be, an obsession with him. Ever since he'd met her when she was just seventeen years old, he had wanted to claim her as his. But the chasm between them was wide, too wide. In his heart, he knew that he wasn't good enough for Emma.

He'd grown up in a rough—often violent—neighborhood, and had quickly learned to survive by his wits and fists. It was a life that was often cruel and unjust. Sure, his friendship with her older brother Ethan had made him an honorary member of the family. The Fairchilds had never treated him any differently because he was poor, but ironically their acceptance had only served to remind him of their different stations in life.

Over the years, seeing Emma blossom into a breathtaking young woman had only intensified his need. While he was struggling to get his business off the ground, she had had a bright, secure future ahead of her. It was sheer torture being invited over to their lavish home and seeing her. Knowing he could never have her.

But she did want you.

Once again, the insidious voice in his head said the words he dared not say out loud. At one time, she'd wanted him. Begged him to take her. But fool that he was—he'd pushed her away.

Luke vividly remembered that fateful afternoon when she cornered him in his shabby studio apartment and began taking off her clothes, offering herself to him. His eyes had glazed over at the sight of her naked body, a youthful goddess sculpted to perfection. One that he wanted to take over and over again.

"I can give you what you need." Her tone, so innocent and serious, had made her that much more desirable. *"I'll do anything, anything for you Luke."*

Such was the confidence of a naïve twenty year old.

"You don't know what you're talking about," he said hoarsely, trying desperately to remain in control of himself, yet unable to turn his gaze from all that nude pink skin.

"Yes I do. I've wanted you since the first day I saw you. I'm not a child anymore." Emma stepped closer, her naked body brushing him. "Teach me Luke. Teach me what you like, how you like it." She wrapped her arms around his neck. "I want you so much. Anything you want, Luke, anything."

With a curse, he pushed her away, even though every instinct he possessed screamed to take what she was offering him. He wanted to fuck her right there and then, and hopefully get her out of his system. He didn't. She was too young, too inexperienced, and he didn't want to hurt her. She wouldn't understand his wants – his needs. He liked his sex intense and rough around the edges.

In the back of his mind, he knew he couldn't have her. He didn't have anything to offer her – nothing to call his own. He was barely scraping by trying to build up a future that might include her one day. Taking her right now would create too damn many complications, but it wouldn't always remain this way. Yeah, as much as he ached to possess her, Emma was his unattainable princess. He had no right to take what she offered – at least, not right now.

"I'm not one of your little boys. I'm a man and I need a real woman," he said roughly. "My needs are different than what a naïve, little girl wants or dreams about. You can't handle what I need, Princess."

"Yes, I can. Why don't you try me Luke?"

"You don't know what you're asking for. Go away, Emma. I don't have time for this crap. Go back to your boring college boyfriends and stick to your own kind."

"I don't want them. I want you."

He shook his head. "Do you Emma? Do you know what you want?"

"I know that I want you. Only you, Luke."

He moved close to her, so close he felt the warmth of her breath, the tips of her breasts through his shirt. "You're so beautiful, but too innocent." His hand came up, sliding over her cheek, coming to rest on her trembling lips as he softly pried them open. He'd rubbed the pouty lower lip, staring in fascination at how it plumped and moistened his finger. "I want to stick my cock in your mouth and watch as you suck me between these beautiful lips, Emma. I want to fuck your mouth – shove my shaft down your throat and watch you love it. I want to come in your mouth and watch you swallow it, not losing a single drop."

Emma was shocked speechless.

His hand drifted lower, down to her neck, and stopped at her breast. "I want to tie you up, bind your hands and legs and have you at my mercy. I want you helpless, helpless but begging me to fuck you. Begging me to stick my cock in your pussy. I won't be tender, I won't be gentle. I'll fuck you each and every way there is for a man to fuck a woman, and then some." His lips lowered to hers, his tongue snaking out to lick her lips.

"Luke," she moaned, as he stared into her eyes. He wanted her to know who was turning her on, who was touching her. Not one of her precious blue-blooded polite little friends, but Luke, the bastard from the wrong side of the tracks.

He palmed her breast, pinching the nipple between thumb and forefinger, a caress too new for her young age, but one that he knew would cause a combination of pleasure and pain to streak through her.

"I want your pussy shaved Emma. It makes you more sensitive. I want you naked when you're around me, with your legs spread wide so I can always see your pussy glistening with your juices. So that you can't lie to me and tell me you're not wet."

Abruptly, he pushed her away.

"You think you can handle that?" he asked mockingly. "You were raised in a mansion with servants, Emma. You were raised to be a proper lady. To be a proper wife to someone who will fuck you once a week. Be the mother of society's next generation of spoiled, little rich kids, an ice princess." His glance flicked at her contemptuously. "What am I Emma? An experiment? Did you think it would be nice to fuck your brother's poor friend, let him experience what it's like to screw between your tender white thighs? No, thanks. You've been teasing my cock for years, all the while dating your boring boyfriends. What's the matter? Are you ready for some rough and tumble fucking?"

Tears slowly coursed down her cheeks at his hurtful words, but she didn't say anything.

Luke steeled himself against the sight, knowing it was better to hurt her now than later. "I'm not a toy, and I'll be damned if I'll provide you with entertainment while you're bored," he sneered. "Leave me the fuck alone."

Emma's huge blue eyes had darkened with pain. She looked bruised, hurt, her eyes full of tears. "I thought you wanted me Luke. I believed in you, but I guess you were the one having fun with me."

He would have to live on those stolen, hurried kisses and caresses they'd shared. His lips quirked into a parody of a smile.

"Babe, I was just having a little fun. Maybe someday I'll take you up on your offer."

Emma pulled on her clothes, wiping her tears. "There will be no someday. Good-bye Luke." With that she'd walked out of his apartment — out of his life — and she'd never looked back — not once. She'd never realized that she left behind a man who hungered every minute of the day for her. A man who wanted her desperately, a man who loved her.

"I'll come back for you someday Emma," he had promised himself. "One day you'll be mine, even if only for one single night."

Luke ran his hands through his hair and closed his eyes at the painful memory. Would he ever forget the tears in her eyes? Would he ever forget the hurt that he had caused her? He rubbed his face tiredly.

The firm slam of his office door brought him back to the present with a small start. Luke looked up to see Sandra, his fifty-something secretary, standing in front of his desk, with her arms crossed.

"You're driving yourself crazy."

He didn't bother to answer, what was the point? She knew everything about him, the good and the bad. Sandra Wesford had been with him since the beginning of his internet company. She'd stuck with him through thick and thin while he struggled to make a success of that first little business. She'd worked alongside him through many late nights — and was there when he'd sold his first company for millions at the height of the internet boom. If there was one person who knew about his obsession with Emma Fairchild, it was her.

"Why don't you go to her?" she asked softly.

At his continued silence, she shook her head. "After all these years, you still stare at that picture. What are you waiting for? Are you just going to sit there and let her marry somebody else?" The challenge in her voice was unmistakable. "The man I know wouldn't sit on his hands while an idiot came strolling by and took the woman he loved."

In spite of himself, Luke grinned.

Sandra was the only person who dared talk to him in that way. He really didn't need her to tell him what to do. He'd already made up his mind as soon as he'd found out that Emma was engaged to somebody else.

It was time to go back and claim what was his.

It was time to take care of some unfinished business.

It was fucking time to make Emma his.

Chapter One

She was engaged. Emma sighed, looking at the sparkling diamond ring on her finger. Why didn't she feel ecstatic, joyful, even…giddy? There was a curious lack of that warm flushed feeling.

Because you don't love him.

No sense in fooling herself. Michael loved her, but he never ignited in her the kind of passion that drove her insane. The kind that made her wet and aroused just thinking about him. No, Michael was more like a friend, a companion. And after dating him for a few months, she'd decided to say yes when he proposed.

What the heck, right? She was tired of dating. Tired of waiting for that one man that would make her burn with one look, melt her senses with one kiss. Every guy she ever dated fell short of the man who had set the bar so high.

Luke.

As always, thoughts of him invoked mixed feelings of anger, longing, bitterness—and a deep-seated desire.

Emma reclined against the huge claw-footed tub filled with scented water and bubbles. Luke Forrester was her greatest weakness. He was the star of her teenage fantasies, her first love. He made her burn, he made her ache. Tall and muscular, rough and rugged, he was sensuality incarnate. The way that man moved, the way that he could undress you with one look, should be outlawed. Her nipples hardened at the thought of his lips.

Those lips—those damn lips—brought forth forbidden thoughts of long, deep kisses and heated sessions of torrid sex. His dark eyes glowed hot with the promise of seduction, his touch sure and confident.

He was a magnet for women. He captured your attention and held it.

He made you want to fuck him, for goodness sake.

Just looking at that sinfully handsome man with the to-die-for-body, sexual knowledge lurking in his eyes, made a woman want to strip and offer herself to him…over and over again.

Emma rubbed her thighs together, feeling the old familiar ache she had lived with for years. Luke was her brother's friend, and from the day Ethan brought him home, she was hooked. One look from those dark, seductive eyes was all it took.

At seventeen, she hadn't really understood the feelings he aroused in her. Now, she recognized it for what it was. Deep, bone-melting, spine-tingling lust.

She'd caught him looking at her once while she sunbathed by the pool during the summer she turned nineteen.

Dark, hot eyes roamed over every curve displayed by the brief bikini she wore, lingering on her breasts. He'd managed to arouse her for the first time. A deep flush had spread over her body. She watched as he avidly followed tiny water drops as the rolled down her front.

Emma bit her lip, aching yet not understanding. She endured his hot gaze for as long as she could before running up to her room. Why the hell was she so jumpy? It was just Luke.

Stripping off her bikini, she examined herself in the full length mirror. She was trying to see what he'd found so fascinating.

Her tender body was starting to fill out.

Cupping her breast, she grasped the hard tip and gently squeezed, closing her eyes at the sharp pleasure she felt. Her other hand drifted over her abdomen, past the light curls down to her vagina.

Filled with curiosity, she slowly inserted her finger in the slit and found that it was creamy with sticky fluid. She moved to her bed, lay down and spread her legs, exploring her body. She discovered her sensitive clitoris; found out that rubbing it around and around gave her pleasure. She wasn't completely naïve — she knew about sex — but nobody had ever touched her there.

That afternoon, she learned to pleasure herself while thinking of Luke. Emma imagined it was him touching her, kissing her. She fantasized it was him rubbing her breasts, running his hands over her body.

Would he perform oral sex on her? Would he tongue her clit and her pussy? She blushed deeply. The words sounded dirty, but felt appropriate somehow.

Emma shivered in the now cool water and brought herself back to the present. *God, how innocent and pathetic I was at nineteen.* Entirely too susceptible to the first sexually experienced man she had met. Luke wasn't like the arrogant boys she knew, who liked to brag about their conquests. Locker room talk, she thought with a snort. Luke was different.

Luke would simply take what he wanted, never needing to ask.

Damn him, he had ruined her for other men. Pushing herself out of the tub, Emma briskly dried herself off. It'd been years since she'd last seen Luke. She was now a grown woman, engaged to be married. There was no sense in indulging in fantasies. But deep inside, there was a part of her that longed for him, longed for the pleasure she knew only he could give her. Pleasure that she had shamelessly begged him to give her.

He didn't want you. Remember? Hadn't she thrown herself at him, only to be rejected? And hadn't she sworn never to talk to him again? Luke Forrester could burn in hell for all she cared.

Emma sighed. That was all in the past. Since then she'd graduated from college and held a good job in the family business. The only thing she'd heard about Luke was that he'd made it big out in the West Coast. He'd started an internet company, built it up, and sold it for a fortune. He was now a multi-millionaire.

Probably married. She didn't know. Didn't want to know, she insisted to herself. His rejection stung deeply, and to this day, she could remember vividly the pain she'd felt at his words, how he'd broken her heart. She could care less now about Luke Forrester. The phone beside her rang. Thankful for the distraction, she picked it up.

"Emma?" It was her best friend Alex. "You didn't forget about our girls' night out tonight. Did you?"

God, she'd been so wrapped up in memories of Luke she'd forgotten the weekly get-together she had with three other girlfriends.

"No, of course not," she denied.

Alex chuckled. "Still mooning over your engagement ring?"

She grinned. "It's kind of stunning, isn't it?"

"It's gorgeous, and you know it. As it should be, since Michael spent a fortune on it."

"Yeah, I know," she agreed quietly.

"There you go again," Alex remarked perceptively. "I have a feeling you're not sure about this."

Alex was always able to read her better than anybody else. "I *am* sure," she countered, pushing Luke out of her mind. "Michael is a great catch. He's handsome, rich, and successful. Not to mention he's one of the most eligible bachelors in the whole country."

"Hmm," her friend mused aloud. "You sound like you're trying to convince yourself."

"Michael proposed, I said yes. End of story."

"All right." There was a short, telling silence before Alex spoke again. "If you need to talk, I'm always here for you."

"I know." Through good times and bad, Alex has been with her but Emma couldn't bring herself to share her memories of Luke.

"Okay, then." Alex's tone was now brisk. "I'll see you at Callahan's in about an hour. Jen and Sara will meet us there." They'd met the two women at college, and had hit it off well, sharing an apartment between the four of them during their years at the university.

Emma said goodbye and hung up. Walking to her closet, she looked at the array of clothes hanging inside. Girls night out was always fun. Pulling a short red sexy outfit off a hanger, she laid it on the bed and got dressed. It was good to spend some time with her friends. Luke was in the past and there he would stay. She wasn't going to waste a minute more thinking about him. She got dressed, eagerly looking forward to spending time with her friends.

The doorbell rang as she was rummaging through her purse for her car keys. Emma glanced at her watch, wondering who it could be. She pulled open the door.

Dressed in a black shirt and black jeans, Luke Forrester leaned against the door, one hand jammed in his pocket.

He looked — dangerous.

Shocked into speechlessness, all she could think was — he looked even better now than he did before. His thick dark hair was cut shorter, but still had that habit of falling over one brow. His face was a study in sensuality, dark eyes paired with sinfully sexy lips that made him irresistible to women. And if all the stories she'd heard over the years were true, he more than lived up to his reputation.

He looked at her with amusement. "Aren't you going to let me in?"

She shouldn't. She should slam the door right in his face. But if she did, it would give him the power, the knowledge that he still mattered. That she'd never forgotten him.

She opened the door wider. "Come in," she invited politely.

He strode in her apartment, looking around casually. Emma lifted her chin, waiting for him to speak. She stood motionless, gripping the doorknob tightly as his gaze slid over her.

"It's been a long time, Emma."

The deep timbre of his voice ran over her like a caress. She nodded warily. "Yes, it has."

He hadn't changed much in four years, she noted silently. If possible, he had grown more attractive. His body was hard and toned, the muscles visible underneath the clothes he wore. Her pulse leaped as he stared at her.

"You're looking well." Emma congratulated herself on sounding cool and composed. Inwardly struggling to control her pulse, she regarded him with what she hoped was polite interest. Luke, on the other hand, made no such pretense, staring at her like a predator at his prey.

"What can I do for you?" *Damn it, where did that huskiness lacing her voice come from? And why did he just continue to stare at her without saying anything?* Suddenly, her dress felt too tight, the neckline too low. She felt too exposed.

Emma made a show of looking pointedly at her watch. *To hell with being polite.* "I was on my way out."

Thick silence descended in the room as Luke stood unmoving. Emma marshaled her defenses, realizing their years apart still hadn't prepared her for the impact of seeing him again.

"You're not thrilled to see me," he concluded with wry amusement.

Emma shrugged, wanting to match his casual attitude. "It's been four years. We didn't part under the best circumstances."

"There was a time when you would have been eager to see me."

Her eyes flashed in irritation. "That was a long time ago. In case you haven't noticed, I've grown up Luke."

The look he gave her seared her skin. "Oh, I've noticed."

She flushed and went on the offensive. "Why are you here Luke? To apologize? I got over you a long time ago."

He frowned. "I hear you're engaged."

Her eyebrow lifted. "I don't see how that concerns you."

"Answer the question."

Emma crossed her arms, anger flaring inside her. She hated feeling so unbalanced—and resented the fact that he so easily did that to her.

Luke stared at the ring glinting on her finger, his eyes flashing something strongly resembling...anger? "So it's true."

The man had quite a set of balls there. "Yes," she snapped tartly, extending her arm. "I have a ring on my finger, Luke. *That* means I'm engaged to be married. In fact, my parents are giving us an engagement party on Friday—you're more than welcome to attend." She gave him a false smile. "I'm sure the whole family would be happy to see you."

He straightened and moved closer to her. Trapped by the door, Emma was unable to move. She swallowed the lump in her throat. "I hate to be rude, but I'm going to have to ask you to leave."

"Why are you marrying him?"

Emma leaned back, feeling hemmed in. She fought to control her body's instinctive reaction to his nearness. The smoldering look in his eyes had an answering heat curling low in her belly, trapping the breath in her lungs. She couldn't stop the shiver that coursed through her. Fire licked at her pussy, the muscles clenching in hot anticipation. Pushing away from the door, she sidestepped around him and edged farther away. "You know what Luke? That's *none* of your business."

He followed her. Gritting her teeth, she strove to put more room between them. It didn't work. He stalked her like some damn hunter. With a deep breath, Emma stood her ground and faced him.

With a light touch, Luke traced the scooped neckline of her dress. She held her breath as he came dangerously close to her nipples. Just like that, the tips visibly hardened beneath the silky material of her dress.

He gave her a faintly mocking smile. "Even now, your nipples recognize my touch."

She pushed his hand away defiantly, trembling. "It's cold in here."

Luke snorted. He abruptly gathered her hands and effortlessly held them behind her back, arching her body toward his. He pushed her dress down and bared her breast.

Emma froze in shock. She was helpless to stop him as he palmed and fondled her. Heat flared instantly in her pussy.

She struggled. His hold on her was firm, though not ungentle. Looking into her eyes, he backed her against the wall. This action pushed her chest out further, making her more accessible to his touch. He lowered his lips and kissed her hungrily. No preliminaries. His mouth just opened on hers, his tongue slipping inside her lips to plunder and conquer.

Emma was swept into a wave of wanting so quick, so sudden, she could only respond to his kiss. Heat pooled in her lower abdomen, settling in her vagina. She had ceased to struggle, all too willing to follow his lead. Luke on a mission was unstoppable. She knew she should stop him, but not yet.

Her eyes drifted shut as he changed the angle of the kiss without breaking contact. The small voice in her head, screaming that she shouldn't let him do this, went unheeded. Emma was lost.

Luke licked a path to the madly beating pulse at the base of her throat. He swooped lower and suckled her breasts, giving her tender little bites before soothing her with his tongue.

She bit her lip, cutting off her moan. *God, she should at least make an attempt to get away from him, right?* Emma levered her lower body in an attempt to put some distance between them.

Big mistake – it only got her into closer contact with him.

"Let me go," she hissed furiously, looking down at him suckling her. Wrong move. The sight of him at her breast transfixed her.

Her nipple came out of his mouth with a soft pop. Emma just couldn't contain the soft moan that escaped her.

"Look at yourself Emma. You're begging for my touch."

Her eyes were helplessly drawn to her distended nipple, wet and swollen. "Damn you, Luke." Her voice was laced with defeat.

His tongue swiped at her nipple again, licking the taut tip before pulling at it. Pleasure swamped her at the touch. Heaviness suffused her limbs. If his body hadn't been anchoring hers, she surely would have melted into a puddle at his feet. Her breasts felt heavy with need, the puckered tips shamelessly begging for attention. He complied, licking and sucking, the stiff areolas fitting perfectly in his mouth.

Emma arched, pushing against him.

Desire was insidious, invading her every pore, calling forth a sudden and total arousal. She could feel the telltale moisture seeping from between her legs.

"Beautiful," he whispered. "Brace your hands behind you," he commanded. Dazed, she hadn't even realized he had let go of her hands and briefly hesitated.

"Do as I say, Emma."

Unable to deny the desire coursing through her veins, she had no choice. Breathing heavily, she followed his instructions.

"Open your legs."

Helplessly, her legs parted. He kneeled down in front of her and pushed the hem of her dress up her thighs.

"No Luke," she protested half-heartedly.

His gaze flew sharply up to meet hers. "Yes."

Emma licked suddenly dry lips. Watching and waiting for what would follow, anticipation rushing through her like molten lava.

"I can smell you. Are you wet?"

She whimpered and shook her head in denial.

"Answer me." The command in his voice was unmistakable.

"Y-yes," she breathed.

He brushed his fingers over the juncture of her thighs, following the sleek line of her underwear over the mound of her pussy. Emma couldn't move. Her mouth went dry as the pad of his finger traced the moisture that soaked through the thin silk. It was glaring proof of her aroused state. With one firm pull, he ripped the underwear from her body. Her eyes widened in shock as he brought it to his nose and breathed deeply. Holding her gaze, he stuffed her thong in his pocket, his eyes returning to her now bared pussy.

"Oh God, Luke. Don't." she whispered, embarrassed, knowing what he saw. A smooth, hairless pussy. Moisture seeped from her slit, making the sensitive skin around it glisten.

"Open your legs wider," he ordered.

"Luke," she protested.

"Do it." Her legs widened further. "You wax it smooth. I like that," he declared softly. With two fingers, he pulled open the folds of her pussy and exposed her stiff clit. He growled in satisfaction.

He slid a finger forward and gathered the moisture he found there. Bringing his finger to her lips, he ordered. "Open."

Her lips opened obediently and suckled his finger.

"Now it's my turn to taste you." With his tongue, he licked her pussy, from the top of her slit to her ass, shouldering her legs apart. Her hands groped the wall behind her, her head tilting back in ecstasy.

He lapped her exposed clit gently, pushing her higher—but never giving her enough to make her come.

Emma moaned as he inserted a finger into her. "Your pussy's just begging to be fucked. Feel how it's grabbing onto me." He started a mind-blowing pumping motion. Her hips followed helplessly.

"Do you want to be fucked Emma? You're so wet; it's dripping down your thighs." He pushed her leg up over his shoulder, sticking his firm tongue in her slit.

Emma moaned, long and deep. *Dear God, he was fucking her with his tongue.*

Just when she was close to coming, Luke pulled back. "What are you doing to me?"

He stood up, cradling his hips between her open legs, fitting his denim covered erection to her open pussy. "I know what you want. I know what you need." He palmed her breasts.

She panted.

"Watch as you fuck my finger."

With dazed fascination, Emma watched as her hips indeed moved, fucking the lone digit he slipped inside her.

"See?" He found her clit and massaged it.

Emma's breath quickened harshly. "Please."

"Please what? Please fuck you? Make you come?" His fingers moved in and out of her sopping pussy.

"Say it," he commanded roughly, rubbing his cock against her.

"Please make me come Luke," she whispered helplessly, too far gone to care about begging.

A rough groan erupted from his lips before he went down on his knees again, pushing his mouth into her pussy. Emma bit off a scream. He stuck his tongue far up into her as he could and ate her without mercy. Emma moved her hips against his mouth, vainly trying to burrow closer to the push and pull motions he made. The sensations built, making her skin hot and tingly. God, she was almost there...Then Luke stopped. Leaving her spread wide open, he straightened.

Emma whimpered in distress.

"Do you beg your fiancé like you're begging me now Emma? Do you beg him to fuck you, to stick his dick in you, to ease the want that is coursing through your whole body?"

She shivered. One more lick would have sent her into oblivion.

"Do you want him like you want me, Emma?"

"Damn you Luke," she sobbed.

"You want me," he declared roughly. "Right now your pussy's just crying out for me, wanting me, needing me. Me, Emma. Not your fiancé." Luke gripped her arms tightly. "Admit it."

Wordlessly she stared back at him. She wanted his lips back on her pussy so bad she was shaking.

"Your legs are still spread wide, your cunt still hungry for my touch. You want me to finish what I started." Once again, his fingers pushed inside her. "I could turn you around and fuck you from behind, watching my cock push in and out of your pussy."

Unfulfilled lust throbbed inside Emma.

Luke gathered her hair in one hand and pulled back, bringing her face up to his. His lips slanted over hers, taking her in a kiss that was neither gentle nor timid. He took without asking, opening her to his marauding tongue. Unable to deny him, she kissed him back, sucking his tongue boldly into her mouth. Dizzy from his kisses, Emma watched him take his place between her legs once more. But this time he meant business as he ate her. He sucked her clit in his mouth, giving it just the right amount of pressure from his teeth to make it throb. Sensations flooded her. She was about to come in his mouth. Emma whimpered, feeling her orgasm build. Her body was an ultra-sensitive instrument of pleasure, totally at his mercy.

Luke bit gently down on her clit.

Emma screamed as she came, trembling violently. He had no mercy, riding out her contractions as she came again and again, finally slumping weakly against him.

"You want me Emma. That's why you're not going to marry your fiancé." He took her hand and placed it on his cock. Unable to resist, she stroked his long length.

"This is what you want. The sooner you admit it, the better," Luke growled. "You will give him his ring back and tell him you can't marry him. Not until we take care of some unfinished business between us."

Still dazed and confused by the huge orgasm that had just slammed into her, Emma looked blankly at him. "W-What are you talking about?"

He brushed his fingers against her still moist lips. "Do you remember that day you came to my apartment and offered yourself to me? I had no choice but to tell you no then. I vowed that the time would come when I would have you in my bed. Beneath me, spread wide open, and just begging to be fucked."

Her mouth fell open in shock.

"That time is now, Emma. You can't marry your fiancé while you have me in your system." His tone was utterly serious "We have to do something about it."

Disbelief coursed through her at his words.

Luke pushed her straps back on her shoulder, giving her breasts one last gentle squeeze. He fixed the hem of her skirt, quickly palming her ass. "Do as I say. Or you won't like the consequences of disobeying."

With one last hard kiss, he pulled open the door and walked out.

Chapter Two

Emma slammed the door of her bedroom so hard her windows actually rattled. Damn his arrogance! The nerve of that man. To eat her pussy, give her the biggest orgasm of her life and then just walk out? That was so like him. Her fists clenched.

Who the hell did he think he was to order her to break off her engagement? Fury almost choked her as she stomped to the bathroom and twisted the shower taps angrily. She hastily pulled off her clothes and stepped under the stinging spray, scrubbing herself vigorously.

He'd had the nerve to take her underwear too. "What does he think he's going to do with it?" she muttered. "Get off while he smells me?"

An image of Luke holding his cock suddenly came to mind. She pictured his strong hand stroking up and down slowly, squeezing and tightening at the tip while he deeply breathed in the scent of her stolen undies. Her face reddened under the steam of the shower.

"Oh God, he wouldn't," she told herself in disbelief. *He would, too.* It would be just like him to get himself off with her thong and brag about it to her.

She snorted in disgust. "Well, he can have it. It's the last thing he'll have from me." He wasn't getting anywhere near her again.

Anger sizzled inside her. Directed at him and at her. Hadn't she learned anything at all? Luke Forrester was bad for her. He'd broken her heart and left her behind. It was infuriating that he still had the power to kiss her senseless and drive her crazy.

It was just the shock of seeing him again after all these years, she insisted to herself. He caught her by surprise, that's all. No other reason.

Still seething, Emma turned the shower off and toweled herself dry. She was no longer in the mood to meet her friends. Damn it! He'd ruined girls night out.

In an angry gesture, she flung the towel on a nearby chair. A glimpse of her reflection on the full length mirror stopped her short. There were faint red marks on the tops and sides of her breasts. In a flash, she remembered the stubble on Luke's cheeks grazing her chest as he kissed her nipples. Once more, familiar sensations washed over her.

"Damn it," she muttered, torn between arousal and frustration. "I don't want to feel this way." But Emma couldn't control the needs of her body. The feeling coursing heavily through her veins was simple—pure, unadulterated lust.

She cupped her breasts. In her mind, it was Luke's strong, graceful hands touching her. She rotated her palms over the pink-tipped crests and squeezed her nipples just the way he liked to. A deep shuddering breath rushed from her lips as her eyes drifted closed. Arousal beat like a heavy drum in her pussy.

Emma lay down on the bed and touched her clit softly. The little nubbin throbbed and stiffened. A quick swipe only whetted her appetite for more. She pushed two fingers in her pussy and bit down on her lip. It felt good. Too good.

Damn Luke to hell. He had awakened dormant desires, feelings she had believed she'd successfully forgotten. Everything she'd done to get over him had just gone down the drain.

Brimming with a combination of arousal and frustration, Emma pulled her bedside drawer open and took out her trusty vibrator. It was a far cry from the real thing but the battery-operated toy would ease her need for the moment.

It would have to do, because Luke Forrester was never going to get the chance to come near her again. Never again.

* * * * *

The following day, Emma stared out the window from behind her desk. The files in front of her sat untouched, her work forgotten. How could she get herself out of this dilemma? Maybe some good old-fashioned sex with her fiancé would alleviate this…this need she had for Luke. But Michael left on a business trip a few days ago and won't be back until the party on Friday.

Michael's call late last night couldn't have come at a worse time. His voice was soothing and pleasant as he told her about his day. Clutching the phone tightly, Emma willed her body to feel for Michael even a small measure of the lust Luke provoked in her. It didn't work. Michael's voice didn't make shivers run over her skin, it didn't leave her trembling. Instead it was friendly and polite. Affectionate.

On the other hand, a host of conflicting emotions attacked her when she thought of Luke. It was a toss up between anger and desire. She couldn't decide whether to kill him or fuck him.

Guilt ate at her for what she had allowed Luke to do. She should've slammed the door in his face and said good riddance. In one fell swoop, he'd destroyed her defenses and got under her skin.

Emma stood up restlessly and rubbed her arms. Luke made her crazy, made her angry. She needed to put him where he belonged—out of her mind and out of her life.

The door opened. Ann, her assistant, poked her head in. "I've got a package here for you." She walked in with a small box wrapped in shiny, expensive-looking silver gift wrap and handed it to her. "Hmm. From your fiancé, I'll bet."

A feeling of warmth suffused her, chasing away her guilt. "I wonder what it is?" she said with a smile.

Ann laughed and headed for the door. "I'll leave you to find out."

Emma nodded absently and barely registered the door closing. Eagerly tearing open the attractive wrapping, she opened the box. She froze. Nestled inside the plain white tissue paper was a pair of velvet lined handcuffs. An embossed card fell out, simply signed *L*.

Her heart pounded, blood pumping heavily through her veins as heat invaded her limbs. Weakness suffused her; she was forced to sit down in her chair. The full meaning of his gift dawned on her. *He wanted to tie her up and fuck her.*

Would that really be so bad? The proverbial voice of temptation whispered the decadent thought in her ear.

Yes! The voice of reason pushed insistently past the thick fog of lust that clouded her brain. She shouldn't even be debating the merits of letting Luke have his way with her. She shouldn't even be thinking about it. Her office phone rang and she picked it up distractedly. "Hello?"

"Did you get the gift I sent you?"

Luke.

"It's disgusting and tasteless."

A low chuckle greeted her statement. "It didn't tempt you? Not even a little?"

"No," she declared in freezing tones.

"Liar," he shot back in husky tones. "Admit it. When you saw the handcuffs, you imagined yourself tied to my bed, naked and crazy with want."

"You're delusional."

"I want to fuck you, Emma." The words he whispered slid over her like a physical caress.

"I'm not into obscene phone calls Luke. I'm going to hang up now."

"Did you tell him?"

His audacity stopped her short. "I have no intention of breaking off my engagement."

"Big mistake," he drawled. All traces of teasing were now gone from his voice.

"Leave me alone, Luke. Find somebody else to play around with. Don't call me again." She hung up the phone with a satisfying slam. The handcuffs sat on her desk. Wanting to put them directly into the trash bin, she could only imagine her humiliation if the cleaning crew ever found them. With a deeply irritated sigh, she pulled open the bottom drawer of her desk and plunked the offending gift out of her sight.

* * * * *

Friday night came none too quickly for Emma. She left work early to get ready for the engagement party. They were expecting over two hundred guests, the crème de la crème of society.

The deep-blue strapless dress she wore gracefully framed her breasts before falling into flirty folds to the tops of her knees. Matching blue strappy high-heels complemented the outfit. Satisfied that she looked her best, she strode into the living room to wait for the limousine Michael sent for her.

At seven o'clock sharp, her doorbell rang. Emma opened her door to a uniformed driver standing on her doorstep.

"Good evening, miss," the tall blonde man said, tipping his cap slightly.

She murmured a reply, a small frown marring her forehead. He wasn't the usual driver Michael sent. "Does James have the night off?" she asked curiously, following him out to the gleaming limousine.

He opened the door with a polite nod. "Yes, miss. I will be your driver tonight."

Emma slid into the plush interior of the limo, leaning back against the inviting leather seats and surveyed the inside of the car. This must be new, she thought. She didn't recognize it at all.

"There are some drinks for you to enjoy miss. Calm the nerves a little before the big party," the driver commented before smoothly rolling up the tinted glass divider.

Emma perused the surprisingly wide selection of drinks on hand and picked one. She really wasn't nervous, but maybe a little wine would help her relax. Choosing an expensive French vintage, she poured some in a crystal goblet and sipped it slowly. The chilled drink slid smoothly down her throat.

The wine was delicious and she quickly finished it. Moments later, she started feeling woozy. *Maybe wine on an empty stomach wasn't such a good idea.* Putting a hand to her suddenly throbbing head, she glanced out the window and took in the unfamiliar sights with a confused frown.

With slightly shaking fingers, she lowered the partition. "Excuse me?" Her voice sounded far away from her ears. Her eyes felt heavy. She could hardly keep them open.

"We seem to be going the wrong way," she managed to get out before everything turned black. Emma slumped back against the seat, unconscious.

* * * * *

With a soft groan, Emma opened her eyes and blinked. Her eyelids felt gritty. Her mouth felt dry as cotton. She gingerly sat up, putting a hand to her throbbing head. What happened? The last thing she remembered was riding in the limo and sipping some wine.

Still fully dressed, she was lying on a makeshift cot set in the middle of the room. The air was a little musty and the walls were lined with boxes and shelves. An old baseball bat and set of golf clubs sat in the corner. There was a wooden staircase on the opposite wall. It appeared she was in a basement. What the hell was going on?

Determined to find out, she scooted to the edge of the cot and eased herself over the side. Her legs wobbled for a second before she steadied herself. Inching her way to the stairs, she climbed the steps to the door and pulled on the knob. It didn't budge. She rattled the door. It was locked.

Emma breathed deeply. *Don't panic.* "Hello? Can anybody hear me?" Putting an ear to the door, she tried vainly to listen for some sign of life outside the door. She heard nothing.

She banged weakly on the door with her hands. "Hello? Please, can anybody hear me? The door is locked," she shouted, trying to stem rising hysteria. Still, there was no response.

Breathing heavily, she walked down the stairs and once again examined her surroundings. There had to be another way out of here. She staggered over to the only window in the room, one that was about five inches wide. Standing on tiptoe, she fiddled with the lock and attempted to push it open. *Damn it!* It was nailed shut. She peered at the darkness outside. With the faint moonlight, all she could see were trees. There was no sign of life anywhere.

She was locked in an unfamiliar room, in unfamiliar surroundings. Fingers of dread clamped tightly around her heart. Her pulse skittered madly. *Oh my god.* She'd been kidnapped!

* * * * *

Minutes—or was it hours—later, Emma plopped down on the bottom step of the stairs, leaning exhaustedly against the banister. She had spent the entire time banging on the door until her hands were sore and her throat dry from screaming for help. Once again she surveyed the basement for any avenue of escape. She must be missing another way out, *something*. Tears came to her eyes. Who would do this? Why her? She angrily wiped her tears away. Nothing would be accomplished by crying. She had to stay focused and think.

Under the cot, partially hidden by the sheet that trailed to the floor, she spied something blue. Clambering to her knees, she crawled on all fours and pulled her evening purse from under the bed.

"Thank you God." Frantically, she flicked it open and dumped the entire contents on the floor. A small sob escaped her. Her cell phone wasn't there.

A shaft of light shone down the stairs as the door opened. The heavy tread of footsteps filled the small room.

Her head swiveled, terrified hope filling her eyes. A tall figure appeared, dressed in jeans and a plain white shirt stretched taut against his powerful chest. One dark eyebrow rose, looking at her crouched on the floor.

Luke.

In that instant, comprehension dawned on her. "You're behind this? You kidnapped me!"

His sensuous lips parted in a small grin. "Nothing quite so dramatic, I assure you."

"I want to get out of here," she demanded.

"You will. Eventually."

"E-Eventually?" Emma sputtered, scrambling to her feet and clenched her fists in fury. "My fiancé is probably looking for me. My whole family is probably worried out of their minds because I missed my own engagement party." Taking a deep calming breath, she tried to stem her rising hysteria as she lifted her chin. "Do you realize the trouble you've put yourself in?"

Luke shrugged. "They probably already received your note saying you needed time to think. To do that, you decided to go away for a few days."

Emma gasped in shock. "What?"

"Your fiancé, I'm sure, will understand your sweetly worded note that said things have progressed too quickly and you have some issues you have to resolve. By the way," he added with a small smile, "you also promised to call him in a few days."

The color drained from her face. "Why are you doing this?"

"Desperate times call for desperate measures." His gaze turned intense, almost burning in its regard. "We have unfinished business. Until that's taken care of, I won't allow another man to have you."

"What are you saying?" Her stomach dipped, but inside, deep inside, Emma knew.

"You were mine from the first day I saw you. Never doubt that." The possession in his voice was unmistakable. His words were outrageous, his gaze steady and unwavering. "You're a woman now; you can give me what I need."

Emma swallowed the lump in her throat. "You're insane."

"The time has come for me to claim what has always been mine."

"So you kidnapped me?" she asked in disbelief.

Luke appeared supremely confident. "It's kidnapping only when I hold you against your will. But you're not unwilling, are you Emma? When I ate your pussy in your apartment, you were moaning desperately to come in my mouth." The heat in his eyes seared her skin. "I can have you begging me in seconds."

Emma shook her head and stepped back, her heart pounding madly. "Let me go, Luke."

"No."

"What do you want from me?" she cried.

"Everything. I want everything from you Emma, and don't you doubt that I'll get it. You're mine," he repeated harshly.

"No," she denied in a small whisper.

His eyes darkened dangerously. "Take off your clothes."

"Go to hell," she retorted angrily, though she moved back two steps for good measure.

"Take them off or I'll tear them off." Luke's voice was deceptively soft, but the warning was clear.

Emma put out a hand. "Don't come near me. I'll scream."

He laughed, a rich, deep sound that filled the room. "Go ahead. Nobody will hear you. We're miles away from the nearest neighbor. Right now, it's only me and you in this big house."

"I'll get away from you the first chance I get," she declared defiantly.

"You can try," he invited mockingly. He gestured to her clothes. "Off."

"And I repeat, you can go to hell Luke."

He took a step towards her, making her move back involuntarily. "I've been there Emma. Hell is to want you and never have you. Hell is sleeping with a woman who has your shade of golden blonde hair, or has the same blue eyes, but who isn't you. That's hell," he growled roughly, heatedly. "Hell is watching you from afar, the need to touch you—to have you—an almost constant physical ache. Hell is having a hunger that is never assuaged, no matter what I do or who I fuck. Because it's not you."

Emma saw naked, unadulterated hunger in his eyes. She shivered. The enormity of her situation began to sink in. Locked away in this basement, she was helpless and under his control.

"The clothes," he ordered once again.

It was insanity to continue defying him, but she'd be damned if she would meekly do as he commanded. "Never."

Luke gave her a mocking grin and edged closer to her. "Do you want me to rip it off of you, Emma? Is that it?"

"Alright," she bit out angrily, stopping his advance. Goaded beyond endurance, she threw him a contemptuous look. "Michael chose this dress and I don't want to ruin it. He loved it on me so much he followed me inside the store's dressing room." She glared at him defiantly, ignoring the warning signs of impending doom. "Do you want to know what we did inside? He fu—"

Her breath came out in a big whoosh as he pulled her against him abruptly, stopping the words in her throat. "Don't push me," Luke warned softly, anger glinting in his eyes. Holding her gaze, he lowered the zipper slowly and deliberately until the silk dress fell into a puddle at her feet. All she had on left was a tiny, blue thong.

His rugged face was carved from stone, immovable and implacable. "Will you do the honors or shall I?"

Seething in silence, Emma glared at him bitterly. Taking a step back, she pushed her thong slowly down her hips and kicked it away. "I don't know who you are anymore. The Luke I knew would never do this."

His casual stance at odds with the lust darkening his gaze. "You never knew me at all."

She snorted in disdain, trying to ignore her body's betraying reaction to his nearness. "So you'll resort to forcing an unwilling woman?"

Luke gave her a sexy, confident smile. "Baby, in a few minutes you'll be begging me."

Emma lifted her chin defiantly. "Never."

"We'll see." He ran a finger lightly up her arm. "From here on out, I want you naked all the time."

Her skin prickled in reaction and she pulled away. When he merely followed, she gritted her teeth in frustration. "Why can't you just leave me alone?"

His fingers trailed down her arms, around her collarbone, over her shoulders. He tipped her chin up, forcing her to look at him. "I'm tired of waiting, Emma. If you're even a little bit honest with yourself, you'll admit you feel the same way."

Caught up in the swirling need in his eyes, Emma trembled with an answering hunger. Heat swept over her, treacherously chasing away the anger she felt. "You can't keep me prisoner here forever."

His thumb ran over her lower lip, quickly slipping inside to swipe at her tongue. "Give me ten days. Submit to me."

Desire flared inside her like a raging firestorm. Her breath caught in her throat. Those words were like a drug, lulling her senses, leaving her susceptible to his spell. Her pussy creamed, weakening her resolve.

"In return for your submission, I'll give you pleasure that you've never felt before." He cupped her breast and pulled gently at her nipple, his touch filling her with treacherous warmth. "For the next ten days, I want to be your pleasure master."

She moaned softly.

"Ten days Emma. Consider it one last fling before you tie yourself down." His voice was persuasive, edged tightly with desire. He slid his hand over the slight swell of her abdomen to the juncture of her thighs. Lightly tracing the smooth lips, his fingers dipped inside her pussy and slipped inside the moist slit.

Emma pulled air into her lungs as pleasure swamped her. Her whole body ached and pulsed deeply. She felt the loss intensely when he abruptly withdrew.

He pushed his fingers in his mouth and licked them hungrily, never releasing her gaze. "Well?"

Emotions churned like mad inside her. Overwhelming desire warred with anger at his gall in simply taking what he wanted. "You had your chance with me, Luke. You turned me down, remember?"

He breathed out. "I've regretted that ever since. Neither of us can deny that we go up in flames every time we so much as look at each other. I'm honest enough to say that I would do anything to have you."

His words mesmerized her. A slow, insidious flame singed every inch of her body in response to the heat in his eyes.

"I would never hurt you," he said softly. "But I won't be gentle. I like my sex rough and intense. A little pain heightens pleasure, sharpens it. I know you can take whatever I give you and return the pleasure tenfold."

His words painted torrid images in her mind, conjuring up visions of bodies moving in unison on tangled sheets. It was sensuous, uninhibited.

"Sex between us would be adventurous. Exciting. Don't you want to feel the thrill of the forbidden?"

Emma shuddered deeply.

"Yes," he exclaimed softly. "You understand me. Give me ten days, Emma. Shed your inhibitions. Give all to me."

She swallowed tightly at the erotic visions that flashed in her head. A small part of her brain still functioned, however, and she voiced the question in the back of her mind. "And if I refuse? Will you take me home?"

His next words challenged her to take the leap. "I'm hoping you'll be honest with yourself and admit that you want this too. If you refuse, then you're not the woman I thought you were."

"And after the ten days are over? What then?"

His eyes grew somber. "I let you go. You marry your fiancé and go on with your life. You'll never see me again." The tight set of his lips drew her gaze as he breathed deeply. "Think about it. I'll be in the study." He turned and walked up the stairs, pulling the door closed behind him.

Emma stood where he left her, nibbling her lower lip. Luke had given her a choice. Stay and he would give her pleasure she never felt before. Go and she would never see him again. What was she going to do? How was she supposed to make up her mind when her feelings were all jumbled and her body pulsed with arousal?

There was no denying that she wanted Luke. It would be so easy to succumb to his spell and give him everything he demanded. She wanted to feel every single glorious sensation of having him inside her. The temptation to throw caution to the winds and say yes was overwhelming. Was she crazy to even consider his proposition? Or would she regret it more if she didn't?

Surely ten days of her life would be nothing compared to a lifetime without him? She'd never see him again—but she'd have her memories. When it came down to it, was there any other choice but to say yes?

Chapter Three

Luke barely managed to control the urge to toss Emma on the narrow cot and fuck her senseless. He forced himself to walk away and give her time to think. In the study, he plopped down on the leather chair behind an intricately carved mahogany table, careful to leave the door open. He stared at the book-lined walls, his thoughts consumed by the woman in the basement. He realized that he had taken a huge gamble with his proposition. Abducting her was one thing, but he wanted her to be a willing participant. He was a selfish man. He wanted everything.

Walking over to the elegant bar in the corner, he poured himself a generous measure of scotch. He had hurt Emma terribly years ago, but at that time, memories of Marisa Tremayne were still fresh in his mind. No matter how much he had tried to convince himself that Emma was nothing like Marisa, his bitterness had poisoned his view of women.

Marisa was a first-class bitch who'd seduced him when he was only eighteen, blinding him with her polish and sophistication. When she seemed to return his affections, he couldn't believe his luck.

He snorted. He was stupid to believe that the only daughter of a wealthy businessman would fall in love with a lowly employee like him.

Then she got pregnant.

Luke tossed the drink back and put the empty glass on the table before sitting down on the wide maroon leather couch against the wall. Marisa had laughed in his face when he offered to marry her, claiming she wasn't even sure the baby was his.

"Oh, Luke. You didn't really think that we — that you and I — were exclusive, did you?" His silence had been answer enough. *"You're such a handsome boy, and I had so much fun. But did you really think we would end up together?"* Her eyes, which he had previously thought were beautiful, turned hard and calculating. *"Daddy would never allow me to marry someone like you."*

"Someone like me?" he had managed to croak through numb lips.

"Frankly you have nothing to offer. People like me don't marry people like you, Luke. It's just not done." He stared at her, for the first time seeing her for what she really was — an ugly, selfish person. *"Money marries money. Trust me, girls like me would never marry a poor, penniless boy like yourself. No matter how gorgeous you are. It's a fact of life."*

He had watched disbelievingly as she'd walked away, calmly getting into her convertible Mercedes without looking back. The next day, she sent him a note saying she'd had an abortion. Deep anger had taken root inside him. He had packed his bags and left, embittered and hardened by the whole experience.

After Marisa, he'd sworn off rich women, preferring those who knew the score, who didn't care that he lived in a small apartment or how much he had in his bank account. Then he met Emma.

Emma was one of the Connecticut Fairchild's. They were an old-money family, synonymous with wealth and power. She was the epitome of class and impeccable breeding, blessed with charm and quiet grace. Not to mention classical good looks and a body that, even at seventeen, showed incredible promise. Emma was a seductress in the making.

In his mind, it was Marisa Tremayne all over again, the same designer clothing and beautiful mansion. She was off-limits. There was no way he was getting anywhere near a rich heiress again.

Luke hadn't counted on the constant temptation she had represented. Every time he saw her, he only wanted her more. Emma would look at him with those deep blue eyes when she thought he wasn't looking and blush whenever he was near. The hunger he felt for her was an ache that wouldn't go away.

It wasn't easy but he'd learned to live with wanting her. Aside from being way out of his league, Emma was too young. Watching her blossom over the years into a beautiful young woman was agonizing. And the parade of *rich* young men whom she dated drove him crazy with jealousy.

Oh, he knew she was attracted to him. He'd have to have been blind not to see it. Every time he wanted to succumb to the urge to take her, all he needed to do was remember who she was and he'd somehow found the strength to resist.

Then Emma did the unexpected. She'd taken the initiative one day and ambushed him in his sparsely furnished apartment. Declaring that she wanted him, she proudly bared her young body. Luke knew he couldn't take what she offered. What did he have to offer her in return? *Nothing at all.*

So that afternoon he'd torn Emma to shreds with cruel and hurtful words, driving her away with tears in her eyes. He'd watched her go, hating himself for hurting her. Images of her naked body constantly haunted his thoughts. A gnawing ache had taken root in him since then. Not even the steady parade of women in his life eased the hunger he felt for Emma.

What a fucking mess. Apparently, unlike her, he was unable to move on until he had her in his bed. In his mind, she was his long before she'd ever met her fiancé. His gaze shifted to the door, willing her to appear. *Would she stay for the ten days he had demanded?* Luke leaned back and rubbed his face. For both their sakes, he hoped she would. Having her in the same house—knowing she wasn't wearing a stitch of clothing—was driving him insane. There was no way he could let her go.

His cock stirred, drawing a small groan from his lips. How many times had he jacked off over the years while thinking of her? Too many times to count. It was ridiculous that a grown man would have to resort to relieving himself in that way. But no woman ever came close to Emma for him.

Behind his closed lids, he pictured her in the basement, furious at finding herself kidnapped. Even defiant and angry, she moved him like no other. She vibrated with life even as her eyes skewered him with daggers. God, she was beautiful.

His hand strayed to the front of his jeans, running up and down his rigid shaft. The image of Emma, naked and trembling while forced to take off her dress, utterly beautiful in her fury, fueled his need.

Luke shifted, his cock pushing against the unyielding denim. He flicked open the button of his jeans and lowered the zipper, freeing his cock. Breathing deeply, he held it in his fisted hand. Thoughts of her flooded his brain, spiking his temperature higher.

Seeing her again after all these years had given him a shock. In the back of his mind, he'd been hoping the time apart would lessen his attraction to her. Boy, was he wrong. If anything, it had only intensified his desire for her. Emma had lost none of the quiet grace and beauty she possessed as a young girl. She'd matured into a self-assured, confident, sexy woman.

He squeezed his cock and ran his hand up and down the stiff length. The young Emma he remembered had turned into a siren with bountiful curves. Her breasts were more than a handful, perfect for him. Her waist dipped sensuously before flaring out to womanly hips.

Luke ran a finger over the drop of moisture balanced on the slit of his cock. Around and around, he circled the head, drowning in the agony of his arousal. He would never forget his first glimpse of her waxed pussy. When did she start doing that? Did she remember that he preferred it that way?

His hand moved up and down faster. Her labia had been pink and puffy, stunning in its baldness. He couldn't wait to slip inside her moist sheath and fuck her—watch his cock move in and out of the slippery channel. Or he could have her straddle him, his shaft reaching deep in her, plumbing her depths.

The leather couch creaked under him, protesting the increasing pace of his hand. Did she even know how easy it was to drive him to the edge? One look at her naked body and he was ready to jump out of his skin. He pulled in a shaky breath. Pleasure was rushing through him, pushed along by the never ending images of a naked

Emma flashing over and over in his mind. He needed to fuck her, be inside her soon. His hand clenched and squeezed. Soon...

* * * * *

In the basement, Emma paced like a caged animal. Could she really say no to the one man she'd wanted all her life? Maybe this was just what she needed. One last torrid fling before she became Mrs. Michael Rutherford. Her last hurrah before she settled down.

Was she crazy?

Or was it even more insane *not* to spend the next ten days with Luke? This way, she'd get him out of her system and move on with her life. She sighed and pushed her hair away from her face. *Was it really so bad to want to give in to his demands?*

Halting in the middle of the room, Emma finally admitted to herself that she still wanted him. If she ever hoped to face any kind of married life with Michael, Luke Forrester must be out of the way. Squaring her shoulders with determination, she went upstairs to search for him. Emerging into a long hallway, she kept walking until she spotted an open door. She stepped through the entrance and froze in her tracks.

Luke sat on the couch, the flaps of his jeans gaping open. His eyes were closed in concentration, his head resting on the back of the couch. Emma's gaze zeroed in on his hand, rhythmically caressing his stiff cock.

Arousal swept over her with brutal force. The sight was unexpected and lustful, and hit her with the impact of a punch in the stomach. His cock was thick and veined, locked in his grip. Like one hypnotized, Emma followed the motions of his hand as it went up and down the rigid shaft.

She swallowed thickly, inhaling a shaky, audible breath.

As if sensing her presence, Luke opened his eyes and met her gaze. There was no embarrassment there, and his hand never ceased moving.

"This is what you do to me Emma. All I have to do is look at you, think of you and I go crazy. I picture you in my mind and I get aroused." His glance flicked briefly on his shaft. "I've lost count of how many times I've relieved myself in this way over the years. Does that shock you?"

Emma bit her lip. "Oh, Luke."

"Have you decided?"

His eyes were calm and watchful. Hers swirled with turbulence and determination. After what seemed like an interminable time, Emma nodded silently.

Luke exhaled sharply. He stood and—with difficulty—eased his zipper over his cock before approaching her. He held out a hand. "I want the ring off."

She glanced at the sparkling ring before slowly working it off her finger. Wordlessly, she handed it to him. He walked over to his desk and opened a drawer, putting the ring in before carefully turning the small key in the lock. Anticipation tore through her. *Now it begins.*

Luke walked towards her and held out his hand. She placed her palm in his, his body heat searing her soft skin. Wordlessly, he led her up a curved staircase and into an elegantly furnished bedroom. Her heart thudded nervously and Emma licked suddenly dry lips. She watched warily as he shut the door and moved closer to her.

Luke cupped her breasts and gently pinched her nipples. Her breath hitched sharply at the contact.

"I love your breasts." He kneaded her flesh. Bending slightly, he tongued the corner of her mouth. Her lips parted in invitation. Luke continued to run his tongue over her lips, coating them with his taste. Emma shuddered.

Unsatisfied, her tongue darted out, quickly meeting his. In response, Luke curved a hand around her nape and pulled her closer, his lips molding hers. He kissed her hungrily, demanding—and getting—a response from her. Luke took her mouth and mastered it, his tongue mimicking the sexual act. Emma moaned softly, moving closer to him until their bodies were melded tightly together.

His hands traveled down the length of her back and pulled her up to his crotch. She leaned closer, running her fingers through the dark strands of his hair.

Luke lifted his head and pulled her hands down. "Go to the bed and lie back against the pillows."

In a daze, Emma obeyed, walking up the steps to the huge bed and laying back against the pillows propped up against the columns of the headboard. She licked her lips, her pulse hammering anxiously.

"Spread your legs."

Emma hesitated. *Submit to me, he'd said. Give all to me.* Her legs opened.

"Wider. Let me see you." She obeyed, knowing that he could see the moisture pooling between her legs.

"Beautiful," he said softly. He sat down on the bed and pulled off his shirt. Emma licked her lips at the sight of his bare chest, the muscles rippling and corded. His stomach was flat and defined. Strong and virile, Luke was sex personified.

"Touch your breasts."

Emma took a deep breath, his softly voiced instructions heightening her arousal. Her hands went to her breasts, but remained still, unmoving.

"You act like you've never touched yourself before, Emma. Touch them and give yourself pleasure."

With a barely contained moan, Emma's rolled her nipples between her fingers. She was so hot she needed to come. Soon.

He seemed to instinctively know what she needed. "Go on."

She sought her clit with one swipe, shuddering at the sensation. Emma slid one finger up her pussy before rubbing her clit softly. She moaned, repeating the action over and over. Her breathing quickened. God, she was so close.

"Not yet," Luke said sharply. Reluctantly, Emma opened her eyes.

His jeans were now undone, his thick cock jutting out in rampant arousal. It pointed straight up, almost touching his navel. She had always assumed he was big, but her imagination had nothing on the real thing. He was beautifully sculpted.

Emma moistened her lips, mesmerized by the motion of his hand going up and down his cock. She wanted to taste him.

His lips curved. "Look inside the drawer. There's something in it for you."

Inside was a huge jelly-like vibrator, soft and warm to the touch. Her cheeks burned.

"Use it."

"Luke—" she started to protest.

"Do it. I want to see you come."

Her body screamed for relief, still achingly aroused. Holding the toy firmly, she turned it on, feeling the soft vibration. *He wanted to see her come, did he?* Intent on giving her body satisfaction, Emma ran the humming phallus lightly over her nipples, before drawing it down to her wet pussy. She drew it around and around the slick lips, teasing herself with light touches, panting softly before gradually pushing it in her slick pussy. Emma whimpered as it filled her, inch by agonizing inch. It probably wasn't as thick or as long as Luke's cock, but it would have to do for now. Her inner muscles clamped down, her pussy filled by the humming toy. She moaned.

"Oh yeah, that's it." His hand never ceased going up and down his cock. Emma continued to pleasure herself with the vibrator, driven higher by the knowledge that Luke was watching her.

She pushed it in to the hilt, the shaft completely disappearing in her pussy. She pulled her lips apart to expose her clitoris, shivering violently at the vibration that hummed against it. Panting, her eyes closed in bliss as she quickly took on a rhythm.

Her hips met the vibrator on its upward stroke, brushing it against her clit with every movement. "Faster," he growled.

Emma fucked herself faster, her hips moving furiously against the cock in her pussy. Animal-like sounds were coming from her lips, her fingers seeking her clit. She was so close.

With every stroke, the vibrator went deeper and harder inside her. The sharp tingling started from her toes and raced up her thighs, signaling her impending orgasm. Intent only on one thing, she moved faster and faster as she fell over the edge, crying out as she came, jamming the toy hard against her clit. Her body bowed as she writhed on the bed.

Gasping, Emma rode out the contractions. She came down gradually to find Luke looking at her. Sweat dotted his brow, and he was breathing harshly. His dark eyes were smoky and turbulent.

"Luke?" Her hips rose off the bed, unconsciously inviting.

He stood up. His cock stood straight out, wet and glistening. "Take the edge off Emma. I've waited too long for you to rush this."

Emma licked her lips as she moved to face him. "Suck it," he ordered.

Tossing the vibrator aside, she knelt on the bed and grasped his cock, licking under the bulbous head. Above her, she heard him inhale sharply. She tongued him all around the tip. He tasted delicious.

"That's it. Lick it all over."

She covered the head, softly sucking before opening wide and taking as much of him as she could. Emma moaned in ecstasy. He tasted tangy and smelled musky — all man. Taking him as deep as she could, Emma held him there for a moment before moving up and down his cock.

He plunged his fingers into her hair, quieting her movements. His eyes glittered hotly. "You like sucking my cock?"

She nodded and continued to lick around and around the head of his cock.

"Then take it," he whispered gutturally. "Take all of it."

Her pussy flooded at his words. Luke didn't miss the way her hips moved restlessly on the bed. "Go ahead. Touch yourself."

Eagerly, her fingers slipped into her pussy, moving in and out. Emma moaned deeply. The only sounds to be heard were Luke's harsh breaths and the wet slurping sounds she made as she sucked him. His hand guided her up and down.

His cock twitched. Emma sucked harder, knowing he was close. She massaged her clit faster. It was incredible, the pleasure swirling in a furious eddy inside her, centered on her pussy. She heard Luke groan a second before his seed blasted strongly in her mouth. She opened wide and swallowed all he had to give. Deep shudders overcame her as she went over the brink with a loud moan. Her hips moved convulsively against her hand as she shook and trembled.

After he came, she licked him all over and cleaned him. She sat back on her heels feeling weak and boneless.

His finger touched the corner of her lips where a drop of his semen remained. He pushed it into her mouth and watched her savor it. Leaving her on the bed, he strode to the bathroom. When Luke came back, he tossed a couple of items on the bed. "That's an anal plug. We'll start you off with a medium-sized one. I want you to use it."

Emma's eyes widened. An anal plug? She looked at the toy on the bed, a strange looking thing with a flat base and a flared bottom that gradually tapered to a blunt tip. A bottle of lubricant sat next to it.

"Don't remove it." With that final bit of warning, he left.

Mortification swamped her. Use an anal plug? He had to be kidding. She'd never used one before and didn't want to start now. She'd never had anal sex and frankly, never even considered doing it. None of her past few sexual partners had even suggested it. *Was he into that kind of thing?* Her cheeks reddened. She *had* agreed to do anything he wanted her to do in the next ten days. Surely, that wasn't going to be part of it? But what if it was?

No way. She was not going to put an anal plug in her ass. Tomorrow she'd set him straight about that. Right now, she just wanted to rest. She was so tired.

Exhaustion seeped through her bones, the emotional upheaval she'd been dealt draining her energy. She dropped the plug and lubricant in the bedside drawer, out of sight. With a deep sigh, she rested her head on the pillow. Within minutes, she was fast asleep.

Chapter Four

෨

Morning dawned clear and cool. Bright sunshine peeked through the lacy curtains, softly caressing her closed eyelids. Coming awake slowly, Emma stretched her arms and legs. Her stomach grumbled, a gentle reminder that she'd had nothing to eat since yesterday afternoon. *I hope he's planning on feeding me.*

She strolled into the bathroom and looked around in appreciation. It was the size of a small bedroom, complete with a sizeable tub and glass enclosed shower big enough for two. She reached in and turned on the taps. Maybe she and Luke could share a shower. Hmm, the decadent multiple shower heads could come in handy. She grinned and stepped under the spray of water. Thoughts of Luke and sex seemed to come naturally. She finished her shower quickly, drying herself off with a towel.

Emma found all sorts of toiletries under the sink. To her surprise, there was even a bottle of her favorite pricey lotion. How did he know what brand she used? Maybe it was a lucky guess on his part. After she smoothed it on, she checked the closet. Empty. She rolled her eyes. Was she supposed to walk around naked the whole time?

Wrapping a thick bath towel around her, she emerged into the bedroom and found Luke waiting for her.

"Hi," he greeted with a warm smile.

Her cheeks flushed at the way he looked at her. "Hi."

"Did you sleep okay?" he asked as he stepped close to her.

She nodded. "Yes, I did."

He bent low and kissed her, his lips gentle and persuasive. Emma yielded immediately, powerless to stop the drugging effect he had on her. Her body curved into his, her belly brushing the awesome erection he sported.

His arm snaked around her, dislodging the towel. He buried his nose in her damp hair. "Did everything go okay?"

Emma blinked in confusion. "Did what go okay?"

Luke's eyes narrowed. He pulled her close, his warm hand skimming down her back and over the plump curve of her buttock. His fingers sought the puckered opening tucked in between the round globes. He froze.

Emma bit her lip.

His lips thinned in displeasure. "You didn't use the plug?"

Emma drew in a nervous breath. "I-I know you told me to put the plug in, but really Luke, I've never done anything like that before," she stammered, "and—"

"You give me no choice Emma," he chided, displeased. "I'm going to have to put it in myself."

His words pulled a shiver from deep within her. What was wrong with her? In the clear light of day, the thought didn't repel her—it brought a sudden rush of excitement. She had a feeling that there wasn't much she wouldn't do for Luke.

"Where is it?" he asked, his voice curt.

She pointed to the drawer and watched as he pulled out the plug and lubricant. He lay the items down on the bed, his movements slow and deliberate. Her breath caught in her throat.

Emma took a step back, torn between temptation and embarrassment. "No, Luke. I've never done anything like this before and I'm not going to start now."

"May I remind you that you agreed to do whatever I want for the next ten days?" His voice was so cold she shivered.

She shook her head. "Not this."

He nodded. "Yes, Emma. This." He held out a hand. "Come here."

Her pulse skittered like crazy. "Don't make me do this."

"Trust me." Luke took a step toward her and pulled her into his arms. He smothered her protest with his lips — slanting them over hers, and plumbing deep in the moist cavern of her mouth.

Emma was unable to resist. He drew her in deep; coaxing her to play and tangle with his tongue. She responded with eagerness, though a small part of her still insisted she fight. But the little voice was drowned out by the pleasure that trickled through her at his touch.

His hands slid down her sides with a light touch. She shivered. His body was big and hot and male. He smelled of soap and aftershave. Emma moved closer, wanting to feel more, to smell more. Heat raced along her spine. Her pulse thudded as her body brushed against his, over and over.

Luke walked her backwards to the bed and followed her down. Emma wrapped her arms around his neck and hung on. She inhaled much needed air when he trailed scorching kisses down her neck to her throat. A moan worked its way past her parted lips.

He bent and licked a nipple, leaving the taut center stiff and moist. Pleasure streaked through her. Her hips arched up and rubbed against him in a mute plea for more.

Large, male fingers gripped her hips and held her steady.

"Luke?"

He turned his attention to her lips once more and gave her a deep kiss before he leaned back. "Do you remember what we agreed on, Emma?"

Her gaze locked on his lips. She tilted her head in an attempt to lure him closer. He leaned out of reach.

"We agreed that you would give me everything for the next ten days." He gave her a brief, unsatisfying kiss. She whimpered softly. "No inhibitions." He kissed her again. "Let go of your fear." Another kiss, longer this time. "Submit to me in every way."

Than and only then did he kiss her deeply. She moaned in surrender.

"When it comes to sex, there is nothing forbidden between us Emma. I intend to explore every avenue of pleasure there is." He rubbed his erection against her, the delightful friction of rough denim against her bare pussy making her catch her breath and open her legs wider.

He settled beside her on the bed. "Turn over."

For a moment she thought of resisting, but changed her mind. Luke was resolute, his jaw tight and his gaze unwavering. Caught in the grip of a powerful desire, she turned over on her stomach. He pushed a pillow under her hips, angling her upwards.

Emma fisted her hands on the sheet.

Anticipation burned through her, making her jump when he drew her hair aside. Luke chuckled. When he skimmed his lips down her nape to the middle of her back, she trembled. He licked and kissed his way down. The bed dipped as he shifted to straddle her.

"Relax."

Emma took a deep breath, trying to slow her galloping heart. She was nervous and excited all at once. What was happening with her? Where was her resistance?

Nowhere to be found.

Luke was a potent force, unstoppable, irresistible. He always had this effect on her. She would do anything he asked.

His lips reached her lower back, caressing the slight dip before moving on to her buttocks. Her pussy clenched hotly. Luke kissed the round globe, his tongue coming out to lick random patterns on her skin. Emma pressed her hips deeper against the soft pillow. He was driving her crazy.

At his muttered order, her legs opened wider. Nervous, she waited breathlessly for his next move. Long moments passed, and silence filled the room. Unable to resist, she looked over her shoulder.

Luke sat back on his haunches, his eyes glued to her exposed backside. With her legs spread wide, Emma knew she was thoroughly exposed. Moisture flooded her slit. She bit her lip. "Luke?"

"You're incredibly beautiful," he rasped. "Soft and pink. Your pussy is moist and shiny." He reached out and fingered her labia. "Puffy right here, begging to be touched."

She groaned.

"You're so responsive." Luke traced her slit, spreading the moisture up to her clenched anus. "And here. I can't wait to take you here, Emma. But you need to get used to having a plug in there, to prepare and stretch you for me."

Her breath caught in her throat.

"When I fuck you here, I want you ready and able to accept me. Do you understand?"

She moaned her assent, lost in his words, hypnotized by the deep timbre of his voice.

Something cold landed on the puckered opening, followed by his fingers. She felt him work around the small orifice, his touch hot and slow. Her mouth went dry. Luke slipped inside past the clenched muscle, his finger burrowing in that secret, forbidden place.

Emma gasped. "Oh."

He worked in a second digit, carefully stretching her. Taking a deep breath, she made an effort to relax.

"Yes, just like that. Let me do all the work."

Easy for him to say. She was spread-eagled on the bed, he was exploring and stretching her in a place she never dreamed of, and he expected her to relax?

In the next instant, she stiffened in shock as the pointed end of the plug slipped in. Her breath caught sharply and stayed stuck in her throat as Luke worked the plug in steadily, until the flat base rested against her tiny opening.

Emma released her breath in slow degrees. There was a feeling of fullness, of deep penetration, stretched wide as she was. The pain that had streaked through her at first had dulled to an insistent throb.

Luke stood up and helped her to her feet. Emma took a moment to steady herself, willing her body to get used to the plug that was now a part of her.

He dipped and captured her lips, at the same time delivering a firm tap to one buttock. "Don't disobey me again. Meet me in the kitchen. I'll make us some breakfast."

Dumbstruck, Emma could only gape at him. Her backside still smarted from the gentle swat he had given her. If she harbored any doubt about how ruthless, how single-minded Luke can be, what happened just dispelled it. The plug lodged in her ass was proof of that. He wasn't a man to be crossed.

Luke hid a satisfied smile as he walked out of the bedroom. Teaching her a lesson in obedience had been very satisfying. The sounds she'd made were sexy and uninhibited, a clear indication of her enjoyment.

He grimaced. He had enjoyed the hell out of it, but it had been hell trying to contain his erection. His cock begged to be appeased, but he had to control himself. Reaching down to adjust himself, he winced at the tight fit of his pants as he walked down the stairs to the kitchen.

He made his way to the kitchen and got some coffee going. With the efficiency of someone who knew his way around the kitchen, he began to prepare breakfast. Whistling under his breath, he deftly whisked the eggs and set the bacon sizzling. He popped a few slices of bread in the toaster and scrambled the eggs. The aroma of freshly brewed coffee filled the air.

Emma walked in just as he was scooping food onto the plates and the toaster pinged. He shot her a grin and held up the plates in his hands. "Breakfast?"

At her nod, he motioned for her to bring the toast and laid down the plates of bacon and eggs on a small table. Before he sat down, Luke pointedly looked at the towel she'd wrapped around herself.

After she deposited the toast on the table, Emma gripped the knot tied above the curves of her breasts in a defensive gesture. "I'm not comfortable walking around naked."

He crossed his arms. "Get used to it."

"Please," she started to say.

"You agreed," he reminded her.

Her face flushed as she thought it over. Luke watched emotions chase each other across her face before she obviously decided that defying him was useless.

She tossed her hair over her shoulder and raised her chin. "Fine," she snapped, removing the towel and flinging it at him.

He uttered a soft chuckle as he caught the towel neatly and tossed it on top of a chair. Bending close to her, Luke gave her a gentle kiss. Gratified by her instant response, he pulled her close. Her response was immediate, her body curving into his. He loved the feel of her naked skin, so smooth and soft to the touch. Rubbing his erection against her belly, he shifted closer. She squirmed when he palmed her ass and kneaded, his hands slipping between the firm cheeks. It was still there. He grinned.

He nibbled on her earlobe before nuzzling her neck. "I love the way you smell."

"H-How did you know what brand of lotion I use?"

He chuckled. "I know everything about you."

Her lids fluttered shut as he pulled her close for a tight hug. Luke held out his hand. Two gold hoops rested on his palm. "These are for you."

"What are these?"

"Let me show you." He held up one hoop, the delicate gold appearing even more fragile between his large fingers. Prying the ends apart, he gently fastened it on her nipple. A flush rose to her cheeks. She looked wide-eyed and shocked.

His gaze was glued to the tip of her breast caught between the prongs. "It's a clip-on nipple ring. I had it specially made for you."

Emma hung onto him, trembling.

"Beautiful," he rasped. "Now for the other one." He fastened the other hoop. Emma expelled a shaky breath as she felt the firm pinch on the distended tip. Her nipples jutted out, proudly showing off the delicate gold hanging on the hardened crests.

"You had them made for me?" she asked faintly.

Luke stared intently at her. Possessiveness flooded him – the desire to proclaim her as his overwhelming. She's wearing *my* nipple rings. *Mine.* He drew in a shaky breath. It was getting more difficult to control his feelings. But he had to. Their time together was limited to a few days. He didn't want to think about that. "Reality is so much better than my imagination." He dipped his head and lapped at her nipple. "Wear them for me."

He shot her another possessive look before he straightened. "Let's eat."

Her body was vibrating like a tightly strung guitar and he expected her to eat? She was still shaken by his gift. A gift he had commissioned just for her. It was such a definite stamp of possession that it made her weak at the knees. Her mind was racing, trying to figure him out. It wasn't easy.

"Eat," he murmured.

With a sigh, Emma sat down gingerly. In this position, the plug penetrated deeper. She winced at the unexpected sensation, taking a deep breath and relaxing her muscles. The food looked and smelled great and she *was* hungry, so she dug in. The eggs were fluffy and the bacon crispy. It was delicious.

The initial self-consciousness she'd felt at being naked was now forgotten. There was something naughty and liberating about having no clothes on. She basked in the hot glances he kept throwing her. Luke didn't bother to hide how much he wanted her. It came through in his every touch, every fleeting caress of his lips. He made her feel sexy and desirable. The air between them turned steamy. Emma found herself succumbing to the spell he wove around her, eagerly accepting his increasingly intimate touches. She glanced longingly at his jeans, the top button casually undone. *He should be naked too.* As he leaned back on his chair and stretched his long legs, he was the epitome of masculinity.

What she needed was a distraction to get her mind off sex. She chewed on her toast and gave him a curious glance. "Where are we?"

"Somewhere upstate."

She rolled her eyes at the deliberately vague answer. "Where upstate?"

"That's all the answer you're getting."

Emma shook her head in exasperation. "What's the big mystery? Look, you haven't given me any clothes, I haven't seen any phones around here and I don't have the faintest idea where we are. I don't intend to go wandering around." She sipped her orange juice before she spoke again. "May I please have my phone back, at least?"

A trace of annoyance passed over his face. "Planning to call your fiancé?"

Michael. It dismayed her to realize she hadn't even given him a thought since she woke up. Even worse, she hadn't devoted two minutes to thinking about him since she'd found herself locked in the room last night. Her earlier euphoria suddenly vanished. "It probably wouldn't be a bad idea to let him know I'm all right."

Luke's eyes narrowed dangerously. "No."

Emma blinked at his vehement tone.

"We agreed," he ground out. "You are *mine* for ten days."

He didn't have to say it out loud but it hovered between them. After ten days, she'd be free to go back to Michael. Emma sighed. "I'm not reneging on our agreement," she countered softly. "But they must be going out of their minds with worry, Luke. Can I at least call my family?"

"Write a note. I'll make sure they get it." Luke picked up his fork and proceeded to eat.

Subject over.

Emma knew when to retreat. It was no use antagonizing him now. She studied his profile as he ate silently. *Was he just going to sulk?* Secretly she was thrilled at his display of jealousy. "Do you own this house?" she asked lightly, determined to draw him out of his foul mood. "From what I've seen so far, it's beautiful. Maybe you can give me a tour later?"

A sensuous smile curved his lips. "Don't worry. Before long, you'll see all the rooms here."

The blatant sexual implication brought a flush to her cheeks. She sipped her orange juice, and met his dark, lust-filled eyes over the rim of the glass. "Have you owned it long?" she persisted.

He shrugged. "I originally bought it for my mother. She took one look at it, said it was too big for her, and promptly moved to a warmer climate."

There was a tug in her heart at his obvious affection for his mother. "How is she?"

"I bought her a condo in a retirement community in Florida. From what she tells me, her social life is very active."

"I'm glad." She knew that Luke's mother had worked very hard to put him through school, and had had to work two, sometimes three, jobs to earn a decent living.

"She deserves it after raising a child on her own, especially one like me," he mused aloud.

"What do you mean?" she asked curiously.

"I was a troublemaker," he revealed. "I got into daily fistfights with kids in the neighborhood."

With her finger, she traced a faded scar from his right eyebrow. "Is that how you got this?"

He nodded. "A sixteen-year-old socked me, right in the eye. The scar was from a ring he wore that he stole off an old lady down the street."

"How old were you?"

"I was ten," he answered. "But I was big for my age. He was the neighborhood bully, you see. I got tired of getting beat up for nothing. I swore I'd fight back and beat the crap out of him. And I did."

"Did he leave you alone after that?"

Luke shook his head. "No. Not at first. He couldn't believe that I'd fought back. So the next day, he and some of his friends waited for me after school. I was outnumbered but I fought like a maniac and managed to scare them off." He grinned in remembrance. "I came home bloodied and bruised. Mom threatened to ship me off to her uncle in Wisconsin if I didn't get my act together."

"I'm sure she's proud of all you've accomplished in life. You're a successful man now."

"She would be proud of me if I was still poor and struggling," His tone was sharp. "Money doesn't equal success in her eyes."

Emma shifted uneasily, aware that she had inadvertently struck a nerve.

"Not everybody is judged by the amount of money they have." His voice turned cold and remote. "Sometimes just surviving is an accomplishment in itself. The amount of money one has hardly matters at all. Not everybody has a trust fund to fall back on," he finished abruptly.

Emma wrung her hands together. He had given her a stark glimpse into his life. "Nobody cared that you grew up poor, Luke. My family has always treated you like you're one of us."

"Others didn't. To them, I was Ethan's poor friend."

There was no doubt in her mind that Luke was telling the truth. Some of their so-called friends were the biggest snobs in the world. She touched his arm soothingly. "That's their problem. Ethan certainly never thought of you that way. And I know I never did."

"I don't give a damn anymore about what other people think about me. I've moved on." He scooted closer to her, his lips lifting in a smile. "I remember the first time I saw you. You were wearing a yellow sundress and a pretty flowered hat. I felt like I'd been punched in the gut," he recalled with a wry smile. His hand rubbed her thigh, warming her instantly.

Heat radiated where he touched her. "You ignored me."

He ventured higher, closer to her pussy. "I couldn't take my eyes off you," he corrected. "You were so beautiful, so graceful. And then you laughed. I wanted to get close to you just to hear you do it again."

His touch was too hot on her skin. Emma shifted, trying to get closer. "I remember. You were wearing a pair of faded jeans and a white shirt." Her voice turned husky. "I had never seen anybody like you before. You looked dangerous."

"That's because you had been surrounded by rich, trust-fund carrying wimps all your life," he drawled mockingly.

Emma smiled and touched his lips, feeling his uneven breathing on the pad of her thumb. "You were rude."

Luke bit down on the fleshy part of her thumb gently. "You kept on staring at me."

"I couldn't help myself."

He skimmed his hand down her side, following the curve of her waist. "I knew right then that I had to stay away from you."

A sigh of pleasure feathered between her parted lips. "I found reasons to stick around when you were visiting."

He groaned softly. "I remember. You were constantly underfoot, tempting me all the time." He parted his legs and pulled her close.

Emma fell willingly into his lap, wrapping her arms around him tightly. "You hid it very well."

Luke scoffed at that. "I don't know how you could have missed it when I was always walking around with the biggest hard-on I've ever had in my life."

She grinned and ran her fingers through his thick, dark hair.

"One day I saw you swimming alone. You had on a tiny red bikini." He nuzzled her cheek. "Like a fool, I stared and drooled. I nearly swallowed my tongue when you came out dripping wet. Your top barely covered these," his hands passed over her breasts, "and when you bent over to pick up a towel, you showed me the tightest piece of ass I had ever seen."

Emma whimpered. She was so wet, any minute now she was going to drip on his thighs.

"I wanted to pick you up, push you against the nearest wall and fuck you like an animal. I almost did before I came to my senses." His arms encircled her and pulled her against him. Heat burned her wherever they touched. "I swore that I would have you someday."

"We kissed that day." Emma squirmed restlessly on his lap. She was dying for his touch.

His smile was infinitely sexy. "Yes we did. Shocked you, didn't I?"

God, she wanted him to kiss her so bad. "I had never been kissed like that before. You were so…"

"Hungry?" he supplied before lowering his lips to her shoulders.

"Uh-huh." She arched her neck, her breath coming in pants.

"I wanted to swallow you whole," he admitted. He kissed the slope of her breast. Emma waited anxiously for him to pull her ringed nipple in his mouth but he skirted the pouting tip. Shifting, she tried to put it in his path but he didn't indulge her.

"I thought I was going to faint," she confessed, watching avidly as he tongued the full curve of her breast.

"I should have fucked you years ago." His wandering lips came close to her nipple but never touched it. She groaned softly in protest.

"I wanted you to," she managed to say.

"Do you remember the summer you came home from college?"

Disappointment roiled through her as he again bypassed her nipple. When she tried to pull him down, he simply took her hands and held them.

"I pretended to play poker with Ethan and some of the guys. I must have lost all the money I had on me that night. I couldn't concentrate because I knew you were out with some boy who was probably pawing you in the back seat of his car."

At the vehemence in his tone, Emma couldn't help but laugh. "Skip Washington took me home, swearing I was a lousy date because I kept on looking at my watch. I couldn't wait to go home because I knew you were there."

His gripped her hips. "It wasn't a coincidence that I was hanging out in the hallway when you got home, you know."

"Really?" she murmured, eyes glued to his lips. *Kiss me.*

His voice deepened. "I almost took you that night. I didn't care if we were inside a dark closet. I just had to have you."

Emma arched against his touch, his hands feathering all over her. "We almost got caught."

"Your housekeeper would've had a heart attack if she'd opened the closet door that night."

With a frustrated sigh, she gave up trying to get him to kiss her and nuzzled his neck instead. "The very next day, you told me to leave you alone." Anguish shadowed her voice. "I was so confused. You blew hot and then cold."

"Shh," he whispered. His lips found her nipple and tongued her through the delicate ring.

Emma shuddered with pleasure. "Luke," she protested. "Don't tease me anymore." She cupped her breast and offered herself to him.

"Oh yeah," he growled before latching onto the sensitive nipple and drawing it deep into the heat of his mouth.

She whimpered. "More."

Heeding her plea, he pulled on her flesh harder and lapped at her through the small hoop. His teeth bore down in a gentle bite, intensifying the pinch of the ring.

Emma straddled his legs and ground her dripping vagina directly over his denim-covered cock. He grabbed her ass and moved her back and forth over him. The friction created delicious ripples of pleasure that radiated from her pussy to her whole body. Her lips sought his and kissed him deeply. She was like a woman possessed, grinding herself on his cock, craving—needing—the contact.

"Yeah, just like that." he whispered. "Are you wet Emma?"

"Oh God, yes." Her hands flew to his jeans, fumbling with the buttons that ran down the front. She sobbed in frustration. His massive erection made the maneuver extremely difficult.

Luke was no help, seeking out her pussy instead. His thumb honed in on her stiffened clit and massaged it, alternating between rough and gentle touches. The pleasure had her senses whirling.

Emma hung on to him when he started a hard rhythm. Emma fucked his hand, audible sucking noises filling the air as her slick pussy lips clamped down on his fingers. "O-Oh."

Despite the chair, she flung her arms and legs around him. This position left her wide open for his touch, something he immediately took advantage of.

"Come for me, Emma." His fingers pushed in and out of her pussy with rapid-fire thrusts.

She whimpered and buried her face in his neck. The ride was quick and furious. Pleasure swirled and eddied inside her, pushing her closer to the edge. A tight fist of sensation knotted deep within her. Suddenly, she threw back her head and moaned deeply. Shudders racked her body as she came. Luke showed no mercy as he pushed her up and over once more, prolonging the intense pleasure. Her heartbeat thundered in her ears as she rode out her orgasm.

He hefted her in his arms and carried her up the stairs, two steps at a time. Slamming the door open, he deposited her on the bed then swiftly got rid of his jeans. His erection sprang free, long and thick. Emma licked her lips in anticipation.

Luke gathered both her hands in his, staring down at her intently.

"Do you trust me?"

For a very brief moment, apprehension filled her but it was soon gone. "Yes."

"I would never hurt you. Do you believe that?"

Her nod was no more than a small jerk of her head. Flames of anticipation licked at her, robbing her of the ability to speak. Her heart hammered, but she sat pliant while he fastened her wrists to the velvet-lined handcuffs attached to the headboard. Luke made short work of her other wrist, before making sure the cuffs weren't fastened too tight. "Comfortable?"

She gave a little pull. The velvet lining protected her and wouldn't chafe her skin. "Yes."

He brushed tendrils of hair away from her cheek. "For so long, I've fantasized about having you like this."

Emma squirmed on the bed, heat zinging through every inch of her body. "Tell me about it," she invited breathlessly.

"In my fantasy, you're tied up and helpless. Naked. Then I fuck you however I want."

She eyed his cock hungrily. *Oh God, I want that too.*

He skimmed her lowered eyelids with firm lips before devouring her mouth. Emma trembled and succumbed to the power of his kiss. His tongue teased, tasted, plundered. Bound to the bed, she moaned in protest when his mouth left hers to trail slowly down her front. He pushed the round globes of her breasts together, the plump mounds erotically decorated with the gold hoops. "You make me crazy."

I make *him* crazy? She was skating on the edge of insanity, handcuffed to the bed, waiting for his next move. Her excitement escalated at his heated gaze and her nipples puckered in the cool air. With the tip of his tongue, he lapped her through the ring. Emma shifted and tried to get closer to him.

His eyes darkened. "Baby, this is a sight I'll never forget. You tied up like this, wearing nothing but my nipple rings." He breathed deeply. "You make me lose control. I just want to push my cock in you over and over until we're both satisfied."

Was it possible to come just from his words? Emma pondered hazily. She spread her legs wantonly, luring him with her pussy. He drank in the sight for a moment, then swooped down and sucked her clit.

Emma reared off the bed with a strangled gasp. "Luke."

His answer was lost in her pussy, his deep voice vibrating against her ultra-sensitive clit. He settled between her legs; his cheeks grazing her inner thighs. There was no place he didn't reach, from the top of her pussy down to her buttocks, brazenly tonguing the small opening of her anus, rimming the base of the anal plug. Her eyes opened in shock even as a moan was wrung from her. Emma gasped in shock. Her rear muscles clenched, the orifice contracting tightly on the plug, pulling it deeper. She felt, rather than heard, his sexy chuckle.

The flat raspy surface of his tongue brushed against her clit at the same time he grasped the plug and began to pull it out. Her breath hitched. The feel of the plug retreating, forcing the muscles to once more give way drove every thought from her mind. She couldn't speak, she could only writhe on the bed and whimper helplessly.

"Feels good, doesn't it?" he murmured, his voice vibrating against her sensitive labia. His fingers feathered over the slick folds, drawing moisture and spreading it around the plug. Then he started pulling it back and forth, in and out, until the broad base slipped out.

"Ahhhh," she moaned.

He pushed it back in, the muscles now pliant and easier to penetrate. Emma sucked in a deep breath, only to lose it in the next second when Luke pulled out the plug once more.

"It's gonna be a whole lot better when it's me up in here. I can't wait," he muttered, his voice low and deep. "Imagine it's me going up here, Emma. I'll be in you so deep you'll feel like I'm a part of you. God, I can't wait until I feel your ass clamping down on my cock, so tight it'll drive me crazy."

"Luke, I want you now," she entreated, raising her hips closer to his lips. His words gave her an erotic idea of how it would look and feel when he finally penetrated her there.

"And you'll have me. We'll take it one step at a time, I'm in no hurry." He licked her again.

The feel of his tongue on her clit was driving her insane. Luke took hold of the plug once more and plunged it deep twice before pulling it out. Emma bucked at the jolt that centered in her pussy and clenched her muscles on the plug, reluctant to let it go.

Luke laughed. "Don't worry, babe. You'll have it back when I'm done with you." He tossed the plug somewhere on the bed before pushing his tongue in her pussy once more and fucking her slit with a relentless rhythm.

"Luke," she gasped.

"Yes. Come in my mouth, I want to taste you," he rasped, his breathing uneven.

Pleasure exploded in a burst of colors. Emma went crazy. She pulled and strained against the handcuffs as she came. Little mewling noises erupted from the back of her throat, strangled sounds of bliss. He rode out her orgasm until the last tremors faded away.

Luke slid up her body, his lips ringed with her juices. "Absolutely delicious," he murmured.

She met his kiss, tasting herself on him, her eyes drifting shut.

"That's just the beginning." Bending low, he skimmed kisses on her sensitive vagina. His touch was light, his fingers briefly dipping in her pussy. Dazed, she felt him part her buttocks. Her breath hitched. He penetrated the hole of her anus, up to the first knuckle. He moved in and out with gentle motions.

Emma released the breath she had been holding. She jerked when his lips found her clit once more. Her hips undulated sinuously on the bed. Soon there were two fingers lodged in her ass, pushing her higher and higher. Low, animal moans erupted from within her, a blatant surrender to the sensation of having her pussy licked and her ass filled.

"Luke," she cried out as her orgasm slammed into her, robbing her of air. The muscle of her anus clamped down rhythmically on his fingers.

He straightened before pushing her legs apart and slipping the broad head of his cock in her pussy. "I need to be in you now."

Emma quivered from head to toe. "Yessssss." She pulled at the restraints, the desire to touch him overwhelming. This was his fantasy, but she was enjoying it immensely.

He pushed in an inch more and groaned. "You're so fucking tight."

"Put it in me, Luke," she begged, shameless. "I want all of you in me now."

He grunted and went in halfway.

"More," she demanded, unable to wait any longer. Trying to draw more of his cock deeper into her, she raised her hips.

He closed his eyes and breathed deeply. "Don't move," he bit out hoarsely.

"I can't help it," she wailed in desperation. "I need you now. Luke!"

"I'm here, baby. I'm right here." With a forceful move, he pushed through her sensitized tissues until he was buried to the hilt.

Emma's lips parted on a harsh breath. He filled every inch of her pussy. "Oh God." She bucked against him. "Fuck me. Now."

Luke withdrew completely before he pushed in again. The smooth slide of his cock made her shiver and tighten her muscles on his thick shaft. She attempted to follow, to draw him in once more but he was determined to control the pace.

"Please," she begged, half-insane, writhing on the bed. She wanted it fast. She wanted it hard. Now. Luke was driving her crazy. His cock went in and out, his eyes glued to her pussy. Emma choked on the pleasure of having him so deep inside her.

"So good," he ground out.

Her breasts jiggled with his every thrust, the gentle pinch on her nipples a constant reminder of the rings he gave her. "Harder. I need more," she pleaded.

His eyes went wild. Luke finally lost control, thrusting so forcefully that he pushed her up the bed, the pillows cushioning her head.

Emma moaned loudly. "Yesss."

The room was filled with the sound of his sweat-slicked body slapping against hers. He panted harshly as he pounded in and out of her pussy, his hands squeezing her breasts, flicking the nipples. Every stroke went deep, his cock kissing her womb.

Emma felt herself nearing another orgasm and pushed her hips harder against his. Her eyes rolled to the back of her head. She was lost in the rushing pleasure, and fell over the precipice. With a soft cry of surrender, she succumbed to the glorious sensation.

Luke groaned roughly as he followed her. Hot seed blasted inside her as her pussy milked him to the last drop. He gently lowered himself on top of her, his breath fanning her cheek.

Exhausted, Emma could barely keep her eyes open. Still handcuffed to the bed, she let oblivion claim her.

Chapter Five

Her arms were no longer bound when she woke up. Luke was sprawled half on top of her, an arm flung over her waist. She turned and observed him relaxed in sleep. His dark hair fell over his brow, his long sooty lashes resting on his cheeks. He looked much younger and devastatingly sexy.

Gently pushing the hair softly away from his forehead, she trailed her fingers down the side of his face to the soft hair covering his arm. The sheet rested low on his hips. *He's beautiful.* Her gaze skimmed a washboard stomach that other men would die for. He was one impressive specimen of a man, she thought, eyeing the soft hair that arrowed down to lovingly frame his erection.

There was nothing soft about him. He was all muscles and steel.

He shifted. The sheet dropped lower, exposing his strong thighs. A shiver ran through her. She was becoming aroused just by looking at him. Her cheeks flamed. *He's turned me into a raving nymphomaniac.*

Her gaze traveled up his body to meet his now opened eyes, still warm and drowsy from sleep.

"Hi."

Emma grinned like a fool. "Hi."

"Checking me out?" he asked teasingly, stroking her arm up and down.

"Uh-huh," she admitted.

"Did I pass inspection?"

Her lips pursed in thought. "Well, I gotta be honest with you. I found some flaws."

His eyebrow rose a notch. "Really? Do tell."

"Let's see," she replied slowly, her finger tapping against her lips in consideration. "Your eyelashes are way too long for a man."

Luke rolled his eyes. "Okay."

"And here," Emma shook her head in mock regret. "Way too full right here." She pointed to his lower lip. "Women pay big bucks to have full lips, you know."

"They're crazy," he murmured, burying his face in her hair.

"Oh, and let's not forget the ass."

He leaned back and frowned at her. "What's wrong with my ass?"

Emma gave him a quick squeeze. "Absolutely nothing," she said with a shriek as he tickled her. She sighed in pleasure as he enclosed her in his arms. "Luke?" she asked softly.

"Hmm?"

"What other fantasies do you have?"

He grinned. "This is one."

"This?" she asked in confusion.

"Waking up with you," he clarified.

She melted. "Oh."

For the first time, Emma feared she wouldn't survive with her heart intact after the ten days were over. Today was only the first—she had nine more to go. How was she supposed to get out of this with her heart unscathed? Suddenly unsure of herself, she burrowed closer to Luke.

In one quick movement, he rolled her under him. "Stop thinking," he ordered. "You promised me ten days and I want every single minute of them. Your mind, body, and spirit, Emma."

Wanting to lighten the mood, Emma stroked his cheek and grinned. "I'm hungry."

"Me too. But I have to do something first." He headed to the bathroom.

She admired his lean but muscular physique, the strong thighs and tapered hips. Her thoughts came to a grinding halt when he came back with the clean plug and lubricant in hand. Her eyes met his.

Luke stood there without speaking, just looked back at her with a watchful and calm expression. *I guess it's inevitable.* Once she gave in to him yesterday and let him put the plug in her, there was no valid reason she could use to refuse him now. With a graceful sigh of surrender, she turned over on her stomach.

No words were needed. He finished the task quickly. Afterwards, Emma didn't move, simply listened to the sound of running water as he washed up. When he came back, Luke pulled on his jeans. "The refrigerator is well-stocked. Why don't we go see what we can make?"

Emma pushed the sheet away, standing up uncertainly until she met Luke's cool gaze. Heaving a put-upon sigh, she lifted her chin and marched to the door. He really did intend to keep her naked. *Impossible man.*

In the kitchen, he looked in the refrigerator and pulled out roast-beef slices. Emma took over from there and made each of them thick sandwiches. They sat down with cool iced tea and ate in companionable silence. After they cleared the table, Emma set about washing the dishes. Luke silently watched her with a thoughtful look in his eyes.

She threw him a puzzled smile. "What?"

He crossed his arms. "You look like you've done this before."

"What? Wash dishes?" she asked with a laugh as she pulled a dish towel from a rack and started drying.

He stared at her like he was trying to work out a puzzle.

"I even know how to cook," she said teasingly. "Imagine that." She put the dishes away and wiped her hands. "I've lived on my own for quite some time now, Luke. I know how to take care of myself."

His gaze lingered thoughtfully on her for a few moments before he ran a hand down her ass. "Wanna go for a swim?"

Emma threw him a teasing look as she turned to walk out of the kitchen. "Is this another one of your fantasies?" Her voice had turned sultry, her gaze warm and inviting.

His lips parted in a sexy smile. "How'd you guess?"

* * * * *

The indoor swimming pool was massive. Thick marble columns lined either side of the pool, and floor-to-ceiling windows afforded a view of the wooded area surrounding the property. Emma dipped a toe in the water, not surprised to find it heated to a pleasant temperature. She entered the pool and floated, enjoying the quiet moment. Water splashed as Luke dove in and surfaced next to her. His grin was infectious, prompting one from her.

"What?" she asked.

"I have very fond memories of you around a swimming pool, you know."

Emma blushed. That was the afternoon she'd caught him ogling her, a day she would never forget. "I remember."

He laughed at her tone. She was the only woman he knew who could sound so prim and proper with an anal plug clenched between her buttocks. He treaded water and circled her. "I'll never forget that day. You came out of the pool, wearing that tiny red bikini, your hair slicked back and your skin glistening with drops of water." Drifting closer, he pulled her into his arms.

She wrapped her legs around his waist. "Are you saying I was the main star of your fantasies?"

His gaze dropped to her lips. "Oh yeah, in various states of undress. The best fantasy of all was of you naked, of course."

"What is it about you and your obsession with keeping me naked all the time?" she asked, unable to resist touching her lips to his.

Luke's grin was wholly male and sexy as hell. "Why bother putting clothes on? They're bound to come off anyway."

A slick thread of arousal shot into her. Emma shivered in response to his heated gaze. "It's not fair. You should be naked too."

His big hands gripped her hips and ground her against his erection. "I don't look half as good as you do."

The stiff crests of her breasts brushed the hard muscles of his chest. She leaned closer and licked his ear, grinning when his arms tightened around her. "Hmm. You like that, huh?"

"I like a lot of things," he rasped.

She drew her tongue down the side of his neck, loving the salty taste of his flesh. "Tell me what you like."

His hands weren't still, roaming around her back and cupping her buttocks. "I like seeing you naked."

With a laugh, she pressed tiny kisses on his tanned shoulder. "Nothing new there. I already know that."

Luke cupped her breast and thumbed her nipple. "Your nipples are delicious. I could suck on them for hours."

A shudder wracked her. "True. What else?"

"Let's not forget your pussy." He skimmed his lips over hers. "Brings me to my knees every time."

Husky laughter erupted from her throat. "Uh-huh." Shifting so that the head of his cock was directly under the slit of her pussy, she rotated her hips. The water aided in the maneuver, enabling to her to do it over and over…

Luke's breath hissed sharply between his teeth. Emma grinned.

"That's it?" Her lips formed an artful pout. "I thought you liked a lot of things about me."

He deliberately brushed against the flat base of the plug. "I like knowing you're wearing a plug for me."

She flushed crimson and didn't say a word.

His breath fanned her cheeks. "No comeback?" Without waiting for an answer, he took her lips and gave her a deep kiss.

Her lids fluttered shut. Lost in the melding of their lips, she felt his cock slipping inside her. A small whimper escaped from deep in her. The fit was tight because of the plug, and his progress was slow. The water aided his entry; her pussy was slick and ready. He pushed in until he was fully sheathed within the yielding tissues of her vagina.

"Damn, it's a tight fit," he muttered, his breath coming faster.

Emma hitched her legs tighter around his waist. "It feels...it feels..."she trailed off, unable to think.

"Yeah. I know," he rasped. He began to thrust in and out, withdrawing until the head of his shaft was at her entrance before plunging back in. His thrusts bumped against the anal plug, making her moan and whimper in helpless abandon.

"Hang on," he bit out, gripping her hips tightly. He increased the pace, pounding in and out of her, his feet steady on the bottom of the pool. The water undulated and splashed over the edge with his movements.

Emma tore her lips from his and buried her face in his neck. "Oh God, Luke," she whispered brokenly, feeling herself splinter into a thousand tiny pieces. Her muscles contracted around his shaft, drawing a pained groan from him. Moments later, he followed her over the edge and thrust home.

* * * * *

Emma sat on the bed, combing out her damp hair. Luke hadn't joined her in the shower, claiming he had a couple of phone calls to make.

Slowly but surely, she was beginning to get to know Luke better. The more she learned about him, the more she liked him. Emma sighed deeply. It only meant that leaving him was going to be that much harder. She looked up as he strolled into the room.

Dropping on the bed next to her, he nuzzled her shoulder. "Sorry about that. Unavoidable stuff." He grimaced. "My secretary left me a couple of urgent messages." He buried his nose in the curve of her neck.

Emma stilled. "Luke?"

"Hmm?" he asked, busy kissing her neck.

"I need to make a phone call," she stated.

He straightened. "No."

"It's very important Luke," she entreated. "I promised I would call and check on her."

He frowned. "No. For the next nine days I want you all to myself. No outside communication with anybody."

Emma bristled at his uncompromising tone. "You're being unreasonable. Aren't you even going to ask who I want to call?"

His dark eyes turned cool. "No need to. Are we going to have a problem about this?"

Emma bit the inside of her cheek in an attempt to hold her temper. "If you would just listen, we wouldn't even be having this conversation."

"I'll be downstairs in the study." And just like that, he walked out of the room.

Emma gaped at his back. That was it? He wouldn't even listen to her? She stomped her foot in frustration. "Stubborn ass. What's wrong with making one phone call?"

Pacing the length of the bedroom, she thought of following him and demanding he listen to her but thought better of it. It would get her nowhere. "This is worse than a prison! At least prisoners get a phone call."

Maybe there was another phone somewhere in the house she could use. She stopped and pursed her lips in thought. He had said he'd be in the study, no doubt doing some work. She probably had a few minutes to look around without being found out.

Quelling the momentary fear she felt, she opened the door and winced at the quick creak that followed. Thank God the plush Oriental runner muffled her footsteps. She looked right and left, eyeing the doors that lined either side of the hallway, trying to decide where to go.

Surely any one of those rooms would have a phone? Approaching the door directly across from her, Emma opened it and quickly stepped inside.

It was another bedroom, but a bit smaller. Her glance swept inside. No phone. "Damn it. Whoever thought in a house as big as this there wouldn't be a phone?" She pulled the door closed and stepped out in the hallway once more.

Emma made her way to the next door on her right and opened it. It was another bedroom. Again, no phone. With a frustrated sigh, she went out and headed for the last door on the right. She poked her head. Aha! It was a small library.

Closing the door behind her, she quickly made her way to the desk in the corner. Her eyes lit up. There was a small phone tucked behind thick leather-bound books that rested on the middle of the desk. Emma picked it up, an excited smile on her face. The smile soon faded, replaced by a frown. The line was dead.

"Tsk. Tsk. You disappoint me Emma. I didn't think you were going to sneak around looking for a phone."

At the sound of Luke's voice, her stomach sank in dismay. *Oh well, might as well face the music.* Deciding to go on the offensive, Emma faced him and lifted her chin. "If you weren't so damn stubborn in refusing to listen to me, I wouldn't have to go behind your back."

His jaw tightened as he advanced toward her. "You shouldn't have done this, Emma."

She took a step back. "Stop right there. Let me explain."

"No explanations. You need to learn to stand by our agreement. No phone calls. No contact with anybody for ten days."

Emma held up a hand. "Now Luke—"

Luke backed her against the desk, went down on his knees and fastened his mouth to her pussy. Shock held her immobile. When she recovered enough to put up a half-hearted struggled, he gripped her hips and held her down. As always, it didn't take long for desire to enslave her senses. She went limp in his arms and willingly fell back over the edge of the desk, opening her legs wide for him.

He was a master at giving pleasure, his tongue an instrument of torture. Delving deep, he sought the secrets of her pussy, thoroughly loving her. It was a fast, exhilarating ride. Within moments, Emma was panting and trembling, on the edge of falling into her orgasm. Her spine tingled, sparks of electricity shot from every nerve ending to quickly render her boneless. He pushed her up, up…then he stopped.

Emma whimpered her protest.

He looked up at her from his place between her legs, running a finger lightly up and down her thigh. She jerked at the touch, her skin too sensitive. His lips quirked, before he licked around and around her clit, never giving her the one caress she wanted the most.

"Luke, please."

His laughter vibrated softly against the pliant tissues of her pussy. Her hips rose off the table, seeking closer contact, but his hands held her down. She clawed and gripped the edge of the table.

Starting the journey once more, Luke aroused her further with long licks and quick laps of his tongue. Emma writhed on the desk, perspiration coating her skin. He was driving her insane, driving her close to the edge…and then he stopped again.

A small sob forced its way between her lips. "Don't do this, Luke."

He suddenly loomed over her. "You have to learn a lesson, Emma. I could go on for a very long time without making you come. Would you like that?"

Biting her lip, she shook her head.

The taut tip of her nipple attracted his attention. He suckled her briefly. "You promise to do as I say?"

"I promise," she said in a faint voice, dazed and hungry for his touch.

"Very well." He gave her a satisfied grin before going down on her once more, honing in on her clit and sucking the stiff nubbin deep into his mouth.

A low, tortured moan erupted from her mouth. Her hips followed his lips, her legs falling open wider for him.

He lapped up her juices and held her clit gently between his teeth.

"Yessss."

A finger found its way inside her slit and pumped deep and fast. Emma raised herself up on her elbows and watched Luke eat her pussy. The sight was the most sensual thing she'd ever seen. Clearly he was lost in the pleasure he found between her thighs. She trembled.

"Ahhh."

He met her gaze, his tongue snaking out to lick her clit. It was so good. Too much, she thought as she shook. He fucked her with his finger and attached his lips to her clit. The combination was devastating. With a keening cry, she came in his mouth. He didn't let go until the tiny tremors that rocked her subsided.

Emma lay on the desk, spent and limp like a rag doll. He reared over her and looked down. "I trust we've come to an understanding?"

She nodded. "I only wanted to make one phone call, that's all."

He grinned at her tenacity, extending a hand to help her up. She went into his arms willingly, leaning into him. "Who were you going to call that was so important anyway?"

"Her name is Daisy Miller." Her eyes softened. "She's a young single mother that I met about two years ago." At his continued silence, she went on. "She was seventeen and pregnant, living on the streets. I found her a place to stay, helped her get through the baby's birth and convinced her to go back to school and get her diploma."

"Is she a charity case?" he drawled.

"She was caught shoplifting at the store." Emma's lips tightened at the memory. "Instead of having her arrested, I stepped in and took her under my wing. She's like a sister to me. Daisy hasn't had it easy, but she has a positive attitude." She looked at him earnestly. "She started her job at Fairchild's a couple of days ago and I promised I'd check in on her. Please?" Her eyes pleaded softly with him. "Just for a few minutes, I promise."

After a moment, he conceded with a small smile. "I'll think about it. Now how about steaks for dinner? Come on."

Happy that he agreed to even think about letting her use the phone, she followed him down the stairs. Luke Forrester might be a hard man, ruthless and determined, but she was sure there was a soft spot in there somewhere. She may have just found it.

Dinner was a quiet affair. Luke grilled the steaks and Emma tossed the salad. Neither of them said much, though he kept shooting glances over to her, trying to figure out what she was thinking. As he lounged on the chair sipping his beer, he looked at her. Thick lustrous hair fell to her shoulders, straight and smooth, shiny under the pale candle light. Her skin looked luminous, soft to the touch. Surprisingly, Emma displayed an amazing capacity for bedroom games. Sex with her wasn't boring; he doubted it ever would be. She was adventurous and passionate, eager and selfless. After her initial objection to the plug, she had let him put it in with a willingness and acceptance which surprised and delighted him. And she was going to settle for a stick in the mud banker like Michael Rutherford? He snorted. He'd bet his right arm she'd be bored within a month.

"What are you thinking about?"

Startled out of his reverie, he met her curious gaze and shrugged. "Nothing important." He pushed back his chair and came around to her side of the table. "Dance with me."

A soft flush colored her cheeks. She placed her hand in his and went willingly. Luke rubbed his thumb across the fleshy mound of her palm, marveling at the perfect way her body fit his. They swayed to the music, the jazzy saxophone providing a sexy background. No words were exchanged, silence filled the room. Emma leaned her head on his chest and seemed content to stay in his arms. Another first.

After a few minutes, he led her to the couch. He fished a small cell-phone out of his pocket and handed it to her, hiding his amusement at her wide-eyed gaze. "Go ahead, make your phone call before I change my mind."

She grabbed the phone and quickly dialed. Luke listened as she talked to Daisy, inquiring about the baby and her new job.

After a few minutes, she hung up and turned to look at him with a grateful smile. "Thank you. That really meant a lot to me."

He gave her a faintly puzzled look. "You really care about her."

She nodded. "Her mother threw her out when she found out she was pregnant. She lived on the streets, surviving on whatever she could get her hands on."

His eyes narrowed. "And the baby's father?"

"Not in the picture," she said with a small shrug. "And she wants to keep it that way. Daisy says she's better off without him."

Just like *his* mother, a woman who'd raised her son on her own. He must have looked so grim that Emma crawled on his lap to soothe his frown away.

"Daisy's on the way to having a stable life for her and her baby. I have no doubt about that."

"She's lucky you're there to help her," he muttered. With her on his lap, he was getting hot fast. Her position put her breasts directly in his line of vision. He pulled on them with gentle fingers, elongating the nipple. "You have great breasts, you know that? Your nipples are plump and tight, perfect for suckling."

She squirmed on his lap, bending low to nuzzle the spot below his ear. Not to be outdone, his hands curved around her buttocks, touching the base of the plug with gentle fingers. She arched against him. His fingers found the warm moisture in her pussy and spread it all over her labia. His eyes flared hotly. "I want you now, just like this. Unbutton my jeans, Emma."

With fingers that weren't quite steady, she struggled to unfasten the jeans stretched tightly over him. His cock sprang free, thick and engorged. Effortlessly lifting her from his lap, Luke slowly impaled her. He gritted his teeth. Being inside her never failed to shake him.

"Oh, yes," she murmured breathlessly.

With his hands firmly on her hips, he started moving her up and down and felt the thick plug through the thin tissue separating the two channels. Her juices trickled down her thigh onto his. The muscle in his jaw ticked like crazy. The feel of Emma plastered against him—her nipples rubbing the soft hairs on his chest—drove him nuts. He clamped a hand on her hip and held her steady for his rough thrusts.

Her muscles clenched on his cock. His teeth snapped together. It was too damn good. The breathless gasps coming from her were music to his ears. "Feel how good it is between us, Emma. Feel how my cock fits your pussy perfectly."

She groaned.

"Your pussy doesn't want to let my cock go. Feel it as I thrust in and out, Emma?" He thrust hard in her. "See? It's clamping down tight. That kills me, drives me to the edge of sanity."

"Incredible," she murmured on a harsh breath. "I can feel every inch of you, Luke."

"That's right, baby. Your pussy is taking every single inch of me." He squeezed the plump globes of her ass together. This lodged the plug deeper in her ass, wringing a harsh gasp from her.

"Yes. Feels good, doesn't it? I can't even begin to tell you how it feels to be in you, so small and tight. That plug is killing me. You make me lose control, babe. All it takes is one thrust and I'm ready to blow."

She ground against him, trying to dislodge the hand clamped on her hip. "Faster, Luke. More."

"Emma, any more and we'll set ourselves on fire."

She whimpered. Luke squeezed her ass again, holding his cock deep inside her. Emma threw her head back and moaned. Then he started the torment all over again, penetrating deeper, plunging deeper.

She bit her lip, crying out as she came, her pussy contracting strongly on his cock. Luke grunted—holding his jaw tight—but didn't slow his pace. He was determined to push her up and over one more time.

"I d-don't think I can, Luke," she whispered.

"One more time babe. Give me one more, right now." He was relentless, pushing her to peak once more. "Here it comes, Emma. Here it comes," he rasped hoarsely before burying his cock deep in her channel and bathing her with his seed. His heart thundered in his chest. Emma slumped over him, her arms still wound tightly around him. *Would he ever get enough of her?* They rested in silence, but the silence was intimate and it felt right. It felt right to be together. His mouth tightened. *Don't remind yourself that she belongs to another man. Don't even think about it.* The end of their ten days would come soon enough.

Chapter Six

All good things must come to an end. Emma knew she should have left well enough alone. But lying in bed next to Luke, she voiced the question burning in the back of her mind.

"Luke? Who's Marisa Tremayne?"

Clearly surprised and pissed, he turned to her. "How do you know about her?"

Emma shrugged. "I heard you and Ethan talking about her before."

Withdrawing from her, he dropped back on the pillow with his eyes closed. "I don't want to talk about her."

"Why not?" she persisted.

"Leave it alone, Emma." His tone was full of warning. One she chose to ignore.

"Why is it that you never tell me anything about yourself? What's with the mystery? Getting to know you is like pulling teeth," she complained.

"I don't want to talk about Marisa." He turned his back to her.

She sighed loudly. "We can't have sex all the time. We can talk too, you know. But how are we supposed to talk when you never answer my questions? You're so closemouthed about yourself. It's not fair. You shut down and walk away. Like that solves anything."

When he faced her once more, his eyes were cold. "I will not talk about Marisa Tremayne. I don't ask you about your fiancé do I?"

Emma got on her knees and faced him. "What do you want to know?"

His response was a slight shake of his head.

Her stomach knotted. "Are you still in love with her? Is that it?"

"Hell, no."

"Then why won't you talk about her?" she challenged. At his continued silence, her frustration mounted. "I want to know you, Luke. I want to understand."

His head swiveled towards her. "She has nothing to do with you and me, Emma."

"If that's true, then there's no harm in telling me about her," she reasoned. One look at his shuttered profile and she resigned herself to not getting an answer. With a disappointed sigh, she plopped back on the bed and turned her back to him, hugging a pillow to her chest.

A thick silence ensued, and the tension mounted. Emma clenched her fists. Men! What was wrong with communicating? Absolutely nothing. Did he think being the strong, silent type was better? Why won't he talk to her? She rolled her eyes. She'd never understand him. He knew everything about her. Knew about Michael, knew about her family. Apart from his mother, she knew next to nothing about him. She didn't stop to analyze why she was so hell bent on getting to know him. What was wrong with that? Here she was, having constant and amazing sex with a man she barely understood. She's known him for years, but not in the personal sense. Was it wrong to want to know what made him tick? Damn it. She wanted to understand Luke Forrester.

"She was a girl I met in Texas."

Will wonders never cease? Emma faced him eagerly. Luke was lying on his back, looking up at the ceiling.

"I never knew my father, you see. When he found out my mother was pregnant, he gave her money to have an abortion." Emma made a small sound of distress. "She refused, packed her bags, and moved out East."

She rubbed her cheek against him in silent comfort.

"Mom was honest with me from the start. I knew what she had gone through. But I was curious about my father. When I turned eighteen, I went to Texas and hired on as a clerk in his company." He took a deep breath. "He had no idea who I was and that was fine with me. I just wanted to meet him."

"He never found out who you were?" she asked curiously.

Luke shook his head. "No. I met Marisa Tremayne during my first week on the job. Her father was my dad's partner."

Emma pursed her lips, realizing she was actually jealous of a woman she had never even met.

"I was working over time one night." Luke had a faraway look in his eyes, lost in his memories. "She seduced me."

She was suddenly annoyed. *Maybe this wasn't such a good idea after all.*

"We started sleeping together every chance we got. A few months later, I found out she was pregnant."

She froze.

"I went to her house intending to do the right thing. There was no way I was letting any child of mine be born illegitimate. But when I asked her to marry me, she laughed in my face."

The bitterness evident in his voice tugged at her heart.

He smiled wryly in remembrance. "She laughed at me and asked what on earth made me think that she would ever marry a poor nobody like me? According to her, I had nothing to offer her. Don't bother asking her parents, she said. She very coolly informed me she'd already made the appointment to have an abortion."

Her heart ached for him. "I'm sorry."

Luke faced her. "I should have known. Marisa informed me that a rich girl would never marry a poor nobody like me. The next day, she got an abortion. I left that same day and came back here. With the help of a small business grant from the government, I started my company. That's when I met Ethan."

"I remember."

"Then I met you," he finished with a small smile.

Then he'd met her, a rich girl just like Marisa Tremayne. A troubling thought occurred to her. "Was she the reason you rejected me?" His silence was all the answer she needed.

That hurt. "Did you think I was like her?"

He heaved a sigh. "Emma," he started to say.

She sat up and shook off his hand. "I was nothing like her. I *am* nothing like her," she said vehemently.

Luke ran a hand through his hair.

Hurt and anger warred inside her. Anger won. *How could he be so stupid?* "You hurt me because of what Marisa

Tremayne did to you?" she asked in disbelief. "I was in love with you. I offered myself to you and you *rejected* me." Emma stood up from the bed and looked down at him. "You broke my heart."

"You were in love with me?" he echoed.

Fury almost choked her. "You judged me by what she did to you. You never gave me a chance to prove to you that I wasn't like her. You thought she and I were the same, just because I was fortunate enough to be born into a family that has money."

Luke held out a hand. "Come back to bed, Emma."

Her fists clenched. "Now that you're rich, I guess its okay to fuck me, is that it?" she asked sarcastically. "Now that you have piles of money, you think you're good enough for a rich girl like me."

His jaw tightened.

"So you *kidnap* me, lock me in this room, and to hell with everybody else." She picked up the nearest pillow and hurled it at him. "You don't care about anybody's feelings but your own. You're a selfish bastard." Her eyes flashed with anger.

"Come here," he gritted out, pinning her with a steely gaze.

"I'm done playing your games. You can go to hell, Luke Forrester. Since you thought I was just like Marisa Tremayne, I'll tell you this." She was breathing harshly, fury driving her. An ache started somewhere in her heart. "You've had your fun with me. But it stops right now. I'll be damned if I let you touch me again." She unfastened the nipple rings and flung them at him contemptuously. "You're still not good enough for me."

She whirled and ran from the room, slamming the door behind her. She hesitated before rushing down the stairs as fast as her bare feet could take her. Her heart thudded as a door slammed above her. Frantic, she entered the first door she saw. Emma ran to the windows, trying to pry them open. They wouldn't even budge.

Behind her, the door slammed open against the wall. Luke stood in the doorway, looking furious. "Don't you ever run from me again."

Clenching her fists, she faced him defiantly across the long length of the shiny mahogany dining table. "I want to go home."

Luke stalked slowly in the room, circling the table. Emma promptly went in the opposite direction.

"Do you hear me? I want to go home," she repeated, careful to keep the table between them.

"No."

"I hate you," she hissed angrily.

"I don't care," he tossed back.

"You're a selfish son of a bitch," she fairly screamed. Grabbing the closest thing to her—which turned out to be an exquisitely carved crystal dolphin—she flung it at him. It crashed against the wall, splintering into a thousand tiny pieces. He cursed soundly.

Emma ran through the door, aware that he was close behind her. She ran up the stairs and into the bedroom, but his long legs ate up the distance between them. Desperate to get away from him, she tried to shut the door behind her.

Luke grunted as his foot caught the door before it slammed shut.

Emma tried to make it to the bathroom but strong arms wrapped around her waist and stopped her short. Struggling mightily, she tried to pry his hands off her waist.

"Stop it," he commanded harshly, gathering her hands in his. Still, she stubbornly wriggled against him, freezing only when his aroused cock nestled in the crack of her ass.

The heat of his body burned through her skin, instantly warming her. Furiously, she fought the reaction. "You're disgusting."

His lips feathered over her shoulders, leaving little trails of heat in its wake. His hand slid up to cup her breast.

Emma closed her eyes tightly, and bit her lip. "Damn you, Luke." Her voice came out in a sob. "Let me go."

He didn't respond, just found her pussy and fingered her. Emma whimpered in defeat. Her anger melted away. She was caught in a dizzying spell; there was no way she could resist. Every breath she took was full of his scent; she was consumed with wanting him. He dominated every thought, every waking minute, an obsession entrenched in her blood. Nothing else mattered when he took her in his arms. Though she hated herself for that weakness, she also reveled in it. She would willingly do what he wanted, whenever he wanted. The pain he inflicted on her years ago still hurt, but in his arms that didn't matter anymore. It only mattered that she was wet and aroused.

He walked her to the bed, keeping her in front of him, her wrists securely held in his. "Get on your knees," he ordered in a voice that brooked no argument. Emma trembled violently as she moved to obey. She gripped the sheet tightly, his harsh breath washing over her.

Luke found her slit and pushed in to the hilt. She whimpered at the incredible pleasure that flowed through her as he pushed in and out of her pussy. Then he stopped. Surprised, Emma looked over her shoulder to see him reach inside the side table and pull out a tube of lubricant. Wide-eyed, she watched him put it on his cock. His eyes never wavered, looking directly at her.

He placed his shaft at the entrance of her ass.

Her breath caught in her throat. Emma was unable to move, feeling the head of his cock pushing in past the gripping muscles. His broad head popped in, stretching, burning, and relieving her all at once.

"Luke," she gasped. The combination of pleasure and pain was unbearable. Her nipples hardened painfully, her pussy contracting sharply. Emma moaned long and low.

She reared back as he pushed in carefully. "Luke!"

His hands tightened on the curves of her ass, pushing in relentlessly until he was sheathed to the hilt.

She was going to die from the sheer pleasure of having him in her ass. He sought her clit and thumbed it sensuously. She pushed her hips against him, lodging him deeper.

Luke groaned, gritted his teeth and began to fuck her.

Emma urged him on, pleading incoherently with him to never stop. Her hands clenched on the sheet as she shifted, raising her hips towards him.

Emma bucked violently. Pushing two fingers in her pussy, he filled both holes, driving her hard toward the precipice. Emma fell on the bed. He followed her, never losing his rhythm, fingers deep in her pussy. He fastened his lips to her neck and sucked her delicate skin.

Unbelievably, Emma felt another orgasm slam into her, sobbing in pleasure. Her inner muscles bore down on his fingers. Dimly, she heard him groan before he came. After the tumult was over, he slumped over her. It was a long while before her breathing calmed down.

Luke carefully disengaged himself, stood up, and headed to the bathroom. Moments later, she heard the water come on. He came back, picked her up and headed for the shower.

In the glass-enclosed cubicle, he smoothed her hair back and tipped her chin up. Pouring a dollop of shampoo in his palm, he worked it into her hair, the motion at once soothing and comforting.

Tears came to her eyes. "Luke—"

"Let me do this for you."

He washed the long length of her hair, smoothing it down her back like a waterfall. Water sluiced from her head down to her toes. With a washcloth, he soaped around her shoulder blades, the gentle rasp of the terry material a pleasant sensation against her skin. His ministrations began to relax her. He rubbed and kneaded all over. By the time he rinsed her off, she was boneless and clinging to him.

Words weren't necessary. They would have ruined the fragile peace that had settled between them. She allowed him to take care of her. She didn't protest when he dried her off and brushed her hair. The reverence of his touch melted her heart. By the time he was done, she was ready to forgive him anything.

Luke carried her back to the bed. He produced the gold rings and fastened them back on her nipples before climbing in beside her. Emma sighed and closed her eyes. Tomorrow they'd talk and settle things between them.

Chapter Seven

Emma was alone when she woke up the next morning. She padded down to the kitchen and found food on the table—but no Luke around. Tightening the towel she'd snagged from the bathroom around her—a deliberate act of rebellion—she munched on a bagel and wondered where he was.

She thought of last night. Memories of last night made her cheeks grow hot. It was amazing how he brought out the wanton in her. With her previous sexual encounters—and there hadn't been many—she'd never even *thought* of taking a man *there*. He had subdued her, and hadn't been that gentle, but he hadn't hurt her. Was there nothing she wouldn't do with him? For him?

As she wandered aimlessly around the house, her mind churned with disturbing thoughts. Every encounter between them was intense and passionate. What made her think she could have this brief fling with Luke and go on to marry Michael? What was worse—how could she avoid comparing the two men? At this point, it seemed impossible. With Luke, sex was intense and wild. With Michael…it was different. They would never singe the sheets. The feelings Michael aroused in her didn't even come close to what Luke made her feel every time he was near. Why had she agreed to marry Michael? Was she condemning herself to a lackluster married life?

On the other hand, she'd be a fool to hope for anything permanent with Luke. He hadn't said anything about forever, hadn't even mentioned the word commitment.

What she needs to do is face the cold hard facts. She needs to just take this time and enjoy it for what it is. A brief, albeit intense, fling before she settled down to marry her fiancé. Unfinished business was what Luke had called it. After the ten days were over, she'd get Luke Forrester out of her life. And maybe, just maybe, she'd learn to forget him.

* * * * *

Day had turned into night and still there was no sign of Luke. Emma sat in the cushioned window enclosure and rested her chin on her knees. She looked out at the clear night, dotted by bright stars. This was where he found her a few minutes later when he strolled into the bedroom.

For a moment, Luke stood there quietly with his hands jammed in his jean pockets. "When I met you, I was still hurting from my experience with Marisa. All I could think of was that it was the same thing all over again."

He held up a hand and sat down next to her. "I know you're nothing like her, but I figured a girl like you couldn't possibly want me. I thought you were just amusing yourself." He picked up her hand and laced his fingers through hers. "I wanted you like I never wanted Marisa—or any other girl, for that matter. That's why I was determined to make something of my life."

"But you didn't even give me a chance to prove that I wasn't like her," Emma countered.

"No, I didn't," he acknowledged quietly. "I was floored by the intensity of what I felt. I drove myself crazy thinking of you. I wanted to see you. I needed to have you.

But I thought I wasn't good enough for you." He ran his thumb around and around her palm. "I know now that I was wrong."

She looked down at their joined hands. The hurt was still there but the bitterness was gone.

"I'm sorry that I hurt you. In my defense, I could only say that I believed I was making the ultimate sacrifice. You were too young, too innocent. If I had taken you the way I wanted to, I would've scared you." He brought her hand to his lips and kissed her wrist. "You needed to grow up and experience life. And I needed to make something of myself, be worthy of you."

"You did make something of yourself," she argued. "But you didn't come back."

"No, I didn't."

Emma looked at him in disbelief. "You still think you're not good enough, is that it?"

"I will never be good enough for you Emma. You're beautiful, inside and out. You're generous and passionate. I don't deserve you." He gathered her into his arms and kissed her tenderly.

She returned his kiss, and closed her eyes to hide her tears. He opened his lips over hers. It was a melding of two souls. They were wiping the slate clean. It didn't take long for the kiss to turn sexual.

Luke picked her up and lay her down on the bed, removing the towel she had wrapped around her. The bright gold nipple rings glinted in the soft lamplight.

Luke pulled off his shirt and unbuttoned his jeans. "You take my breath away." He bent low and skimmed his lips over her quivering breasts. He pulled a tip into his mouth and suckled firmly.

She cupped his heavy testicles before gliding her hand up to his erect cock. She encircled it, catching the drop of moisture at the slit with her finger. His eyes gleamed as she brought the finger to her lips and tasted him.

Raising herself on her elbows, Emma took him in her mouth. He threw his head back, his eyes closing.

She licked the broad head. "I love the way you taste."

"You're killing me," he whispered hoarsely, gentling her movements until she stopped. He sat on the bed and positioned her on top of him. With her knees on either side of his hips, she reached for his cock and guided him inside her. She trembled as she impaled herself.

Emma followed where he led, wrapping her arms around him, completely in tune with his gentle pace. This time it was different. It was emotional. A tear rolled down her cheek.

He brushed it away, and kissed her again and again. "I can't change what happened in the past but I want you to know I regret hurting you," he whispered. "If I could keep you with me here forever, I would."

Her heart broke at his words. He ran his hand up and down her back in soothing motions. Emma buried her face in his neck. She trembled and came the same time he did, their mutual orgasm a rolling wave of calm release.

She was still in love with Luke Forrester.

* * * * *

Emma awoke tender and sore in certain places. Luke had taken her again and again last night, barely giving her time to rest before starting again. She sat up and pushed the sheet out of the way.

Today, she and Luke were going to have a serious talk. Enough time had been wasted. She had finally come to terms with her feelings for him and she intended to tell him how she felt. She stretched her arms above her head, and then froze. Her blue strapless dress and her purse lay at the foot of the bed. Her pulse jumped in fear. It could only mean one thing.

No!

Wrapping the sheet haphazardly around her, she raced down the stairs. She checked in the kitchen. Empty. She raced to the study. Empty as well. Her heart sank as she went from room to room. Luke was gone.

A uniformed chauffeur stood by the front door, his cap in his hand. Emma stopped short when she saw him. It was the same driver who had brought her here.

"Where is he?" she asked hoarsely.

The man politely lowered his eyes. "My orders are to take you home, miss."

She wanted to roar in frustration. "Where is he?" she demanded.

He shook his head. "I don't know, miss."

Emma glimpsed pity in his otherwise expressionless face and winced. Her back stiffened and she squared her shoulders. She wasn't about to break down in front of him. "Very well. I should be ready to go in a few minutes." Without looking back, she went back up the stairs.

She tore the sheet off and flung it on the bed. A sob broke from her and she pressed her hands tightly against her eyes. "Damn you, Luke."

He had left her again.

* * * * *

Her machine blinked accusingly at her, the red flashing light indicating she had thirty messages. Emma ignored it and made a beeline for her bedroom. Exhaustion dogged her steps, physical as well as emotional. The first phone call she made was to her mother. In a quiet voice, she said she was home and would explain everything later. Ethan got on the phone and demanded she come over to explain right away. She said no. Much as she loved her brother, she couldn't take his probing questions right now. Somewhat curtly, she told him that she would see them all in the next couple of days.

The next phone call she made was more difficult. When Michael came on the line, a heavy feeling settled over her. The last thing she wanted to do was hurt him, but there was no way around it. After she apologized for disappearing the way she had, she informed him they needed to talk. He agreed and promised to be at her apartment in the next hour.

A shower and a change of clothes refreshed her. The doorbell rang. Michael stood there, neatly dressed in a suit and tie, looking somewhat unsure of himself as he stepped inside. She felt a tug of guilt at what she was about to do.

The look he gave her was quietly probing. "You're looking well. Is everything alright, Emma?"

She took his hand and led him to the sofa. "Michael, I think it would be a terrible mistake for us to get married."

He searched her eyes. "Why?"

Her smile was wistful. "You and I don't really love each other. We're much better off as friends."

Michael smiled wryly. "We like the same things and we get along very well. I say that's more than what most other married people have. "

"We'd bore each other within months."

He squeezed her hand. "Are you sure, Emma? Maybe it's just pre-wedding jitters."

He was so sweet. The last thing she wanted to do was hurt him. "You deserve more than I could give you. Some other woman would be lucky to have you." Pulling off the engagement ring, she handed it back to him.

"I bought it for you. It's yours." His eyes were enigmatic, dark and unreadable. "Do you want to tell me what happened?"

"My heart just isn't in it. Forgive me, Michael."

"There's nothing to forgive," he reassured her. There was no emotion in his eyes, no clue as to what he really felt. Emma was relieved when he left, the guilt she had felt was assuaged. Marrying him really would've been a big mistake. It was the hardest thing she'd ever had to do but she was never more certain of anything in her life. Now it was time to find Luke.

She picked up the phone and did some digging for Luke's office phone number. When she called, she was told he wasn't available. Seething with frustration, she slammed the phone down. This was the last time he'd ever leave her, she promised herself. When she got a hold of him, she would make him admit that he loved her too. But first, she had to track him down. And she knew the perfect person to help her. Alex.

Alex answered on the second ring and was relieved to hear her voice.

"I need to see you," Emma said simply.

"I'll be there in a few minutes," Alex replied. When she arrived, she gave Emma a hug. "You okay?"

Emma took a deep breath and told her the whole story.

Alex grinned. "Interesting. Kinky, too."

Emma gave a brief laugh then sobered. "I broke it off with Michael."

"Probably for the best under the circumstances," Alex commented dryly, ever the pragmatist.

She paced back and forth in front of her friend. "I don't know what to do, Alex. He left me again."

Alex's gaze was sharp, assessing. "What do you want to do?"

"Whatever I have to do to get him back. I love him."

Two perfectly shaped eyebrows rose. "I have an idea—but you have to be very sure about this. Are you?"

Emma didn't even hesitate. "Absolutely."

Her best friend grinned. "Then let's get to work. We have a lot of things to do."

* * * * *

The elevator doors opened directly into the marble foyer of his penthouse. Recessed lights bathed the entryway in their soft, relaxing glow. Luke walked in and dropped his car keys on a side table. The silence was deafening. He sighed. He was getting sick of coming home to an empty house.

His glance flicked on the pile of mail but he strode past it and tossed his coat on the back of a chair. With impatient fingers, he loosened his tie and headed for the fully stocked refrigerator in the kitchen. He grabbed a beer, twisted off the cap, and took a long, healthy gulp.

He made his way to the French doors that led to the terrace. The air was cold but he didn't care. Muted sounds of the early evening traffic down below reached him. He leaned over the railing and looked out at the city lights.

I wonder what she's doing right now. Or who she's doing it with. The last thought didn't sit well with him. He was getting very adept at avoiding any thought of Emma with her fiancé. He snorted. When the hell was he going to get it through his thick head that she wasn't his?

He pressed his fingers against his eyes tightly. Maybe someday he'd forget about her. But not tonight. The memories were too fresh. That's all he would ever have of her, the fucking memories of their time together. They'd just have to last him a lifetime.

With a heavy sigh, he went back in and left the empty beer bottle on the sink before walking down the dark hallway into his bedroom. He didn't bother to turn on the light, instead heading directly to the walk-in closet and pulling off his clothes.

His neatly pressed tuxedo for the charity dinner tonight hung in the corner. He didn't want to go. The last thing he wanted to do was to schmooze with people he could care less about. Maybe it was time to take a vacation, or seriously think about moving somewhere else. It was time to get away and try to forget Emma.

He ran his hands through his hair. Pathetic, that's what he was. Mooning over an engaged woman like a lovesick puppy. He emerged from the closet into his bedroom and flicked on the light switch. Luke froze at the sight that greeted him.

Emma lay on the king-sized bed, her hands bound by red silk scarves above her head. Her legs were similarly bound to the end of the bed.

He was unable to take his eyes off the delectable curves of her body. "What are you doing here?"

"Offering myself to you," she answered in a husky voice.

His gaze raked over her. Her breasts stood proud and full, the tips puckered and stiff with the help of his nipple rings. Any attempt to clear his fuzzy brain failed. His body and mind were now focused on fucking her.

"I want *you*, not Michael. I knew I could never marry him after spending time with you."

Her words brought him back to life. "Tell me you're mine," he growled.

"I'm yours if you want me."

He couldn't remember a time when he didn't want her. "Oh I want you alright. From here on out there's no turning back, Emma." His eyes glittered hotly as he gazed at the erotic picture she made, bound for him. "I will never let you go."

Hurt shadowed her blue eyes. "Are *you* sure Luke? I don't think I can take it if you leave me again."

Luke pushed a tendril of hair away from her cheek, hating the vulnerability in her tone. "I shouldn't have left you. But I felt like I had no right to stay with you, to keep you with me." His finger rubbed against her lips. "I'm glad you're here."

Her tongue darted out to taste him. "Here I am. Take me Luke."

Resting his hand on the slight swell of her belly, he teased her with light, sensuous touches. "You look incredibly beautiful tied up on my bed," he whispered against her neck. He kneaded her breast softly, his thumb brushing her nipple.

The urge to fuck her was overwhelming. He slid a hand to the curve of her hip and tongued her ringed nipple. "Just looking at you makes my mouth water. I love the way you taste."

He nuzzled her breast. "I haven't had any sleep since I left you," he murmured. "I drove myself crazy thinking that another man had the right to touch you, to kiss you, to fuck you."

Emma writhed on the bed. "I don't want anybody but you."

His lips feathered over the gentle swell of her stomach before gliding lower. He licked teasingly at the very top of her slit. "Delicious."

"Luke," she gasped, tossing her head on the pillow.

He gently parted the puffy lips and exposed her moist pink flesh, the stiff nubbin of her clitoris glistening wetly. He licked it slowly.

Emma licked her lips. "Will the master allow his slave to pleasure him?" His pulse jumped in excitement. He shot her a wicked smile. "What did the slave have in mind?"

Her tongue appeared between her lips as she stared at his cock. "The slave would like to suck her master between her lips."

"She would, would she?" he murmured, his cock twitching at her words. Placing his knees on either side of her, he balanced his weight on the bed. The two pillows underneath her head positioned her mouth perfectly for his cock.

"Pleasure me slave," he commanded hoarsely, mesmerized by the sight of her looking hungrily at his cock.

"Thank you, master." She placed her lips over the head and took him in her mouth.

His nostrils flared as he pulled in a deep breath. He wanted nothing more than to push his whole length into her. He cradled her head gently, unable to take his eyes off her lips as they stretched over his cock. He bent over her, placing one palm flat against the headboard, moving his hips in time to the movement of her head. Sweat broke out on his skin, his body trembling with the effort to hold onto control. God knows how long he would last — the pleasure was killing him.

"Suck, Emma. Suck me deep in your mouth."

She took him deep and released him in slow degrees. On the way up, she quickly swiped the underside of his cock with her tongue. She repeated the movement again and again. Luke trembled. "Baby, I'm not gonna last."

She sucked the head and licked around and around. "So let go," she invited.

His eyes closed in defeat. Angling her head, he pumped his hips in the hot, moist cavern of her mouth. It felt fantastic. Pleasure shot from the base of his spine. He shuddered. "I'm gonna come."

She never stopped licking. Luke growled deeply. It was the only warning she got before he shot his semen deep into her mouth. Her eyes met his as she swallowed the salty liquid he splashed against the back of her throat.

His body shook, the powerful orgasm going on and on, until the very last shudder was wrung out of him.

Afterwards, he carefully moved from his position and glanced down at her. "Get ready for more."

Luke moved over her and sucked a nipple into his mouth. He bit gently down on the tip, adding to the pressure of the nipple ring. Emma uttered a low moan, her hips coming off the bed.

"You're so responsive to my touch." Immense satisfaction rolled through him. He reared up and captured her lips, taking them in an erotic open-mouthed kiss. Her breath became his, the power of the kiss infusing him with pleasure.

Luke slid down her body and placed his lips between her legs. His tongue became an instrument of torture and pleasure, the stiffened flesh discovering the secret hollows of her pussy, leaving no part untouched, no place unexplored. He pulled the clit and sucked deeply.

"Luke," she gasped.

Reaching into the drawer next to the bed, he took out an anal plug that was quite a bit larger than the one he'd previously used. He caught her wide-eyed gaze. He calmly spread a thick line of lubrication from tip to bottom.

With a quick flick of his wrist, Luke released her legs from the silk scarves and spread them wide. The tip of the plug slowly penetrated the tight muscles of her anus. The lubrication eased the way and the plug made slow, gentle progress inside her. The gradual flaring shape stretched her, provoking a low animal moan from her throat. Emma whimpered and strained against the scarves binding her arms.

Luke's eyes glittered hotly as he watched the plug slip in entirely, its base resting against the entrance to her ass. His harsh breaths echoed loudly in the room as he positioned his cock at the slick opening of her pussy and slipped in. Her earthy moan reached his ears.

He gritted his teeth. "Christ," he muttered. "You're so tight." He pushed his cock insistently in her, forcing her sensitive tissues to make room for his thick length until he was seated to the hilt.

The tight fit enveloped his cock like a glove as he pumped in and out. "Jesus, it feels incredible." His whole body clenched, slick with perspiration. Slivers of pleasure coiled around his cock, pulling the skin of his testicles tight. He clamped his jaw at the electricity charging up his spine. He was ready to explode. He groaned, mesmerized by her hips arching hungrily against his. His hips slammed against hers, his balls slapping against the base of the plug. With each brutal thrust, the plug slid deeper in her ass. The large plug left him little room to maneuver. Luke shook with the effort to control himself. He didn't want to come yet. He wanted it to last.

"Oh God," she sobbed. "Harder. Fuck me harder, Luke." She repeated his name over and over, begging him not to stop.

He was past the point of caring. Pleasure slammed into him as he plumbed the depths of her pussy. He smothered her scream with a kiss, helpless in the grip of a powerful orgasm. Emma was lost in the throes of her own release, writhing in his arms. He rode out the sensations, locked against her as the shudders turned into a gentle trembling before finally receding. He reached up to release her arms and buried his face in the fragrance of her hair.

He felt shattered, weak, and satisfied. Only with Emma was sex this good, this exhilarating.

He gathered her close as he settled next to her. "I'm sorry for the way I left."

Emma cupped his face. "I love *you*, whether you're rich or poor. I am nothing like Marisa Tremayne. I would love to have your child—and I'll shout it from the rooftops if that's what it takes to convince you."

His heart expanded at her words. The truth had always been there. He had just been too blind to see it.

Tears came to her eyes. "But I don't think I can take it if you leave me again."

He hated himself at that moment for all the hurt he'd inflicted on her. "I'll never leave you again. I'm sorry for hurting you, for leaving you and breaking your heart. Twice," he whispered, wiping away the tears from her cheeks. "I was a fool."

She turned her face into his palm and kissed him. "I've always been yours, Luke."

"I still don't deserve you. You're generous, giving, and passionate." He looked into her eyes. "I love you."

He kissed her, pouring all the love he felt for her into it—no longer afraid of what she made him feel. Love suffused him as he held her in his arms. He was finally home.

After a few moments, he threw her a curious look. "How did you manage to get in here?"

Emma grinned. "With a little help from your secretary and Alex."

Luke laughed. "I think I'll be giving Sandy a huge raise—starting tomorrow." He hugged her close, feeling happy and contented. Emma was now his.

Epilogue

"When do you think we can slip away?"

Emma giggled. "You can't leave your own wedding reception, Luke."

He wrapped his arm around her waist. "There's tons of food, the band's playing great music, and the people are schmoozing. They'll be too busy to miss us."

She tapped him on the arm. "Stop it."

Luke nuzzled her neck. "But I've been wondering what you have on under your wedding dress. It's been driving me crazy all day."

"You kissed me before the priest said you could."

He was unrepentant. "He was taking too long."

Emma was so happy she could burst. Their wedding had been perfect. The sun had finally come out after days of continuous rain, the ceremony had gone off without a hitch, and all of their loved ones and close friends were present. She grinned. If she hadn't talked him out of it, he would have flown her to Vegas months ago and married her on the spot. He hadn't wanted to wait long enough for a ceremony.

Her family was happy that they were together, although her mother wasn't too thrilled at having only two months to organize a proper wedding. But Luke wouldn't relent; he'd been determined to marry her right away. Her mother had been a little dynamo, whipping everybody into shape and managing to arrange a wonderful garden wedding. The ceremony had been simple, yet touching, bringing tears to Emma's eyes. Today she'd become Mrs. Luke Forrester.

"Have I told you that you looked ravishing today?" he murmured in her ear.

She smiled. "Only about a dozen times. And take your hand off my behind."

He laughed, the tone husky and intimate. "You can't blame me. I've been having visions of you wearing a red garter belt with little hearts and a matching sexy red bra."

"Ahhh, but you're wrong."

His eyebrow rose. "Blue garter belt and matching bra?"

With a naughty grin, she pulled him down to whisper in his ear. He groaned. "You're killing me here Emma."

They pulled apart as guests came up and congratulated them before moving on. She looked around and spotted her brother Ethan dancing with her best friend Alex in the traditional best man and maid of honor dance. She noted the strained look on her brother's face. Alex, she noticed, was radiant as she danced with Ethan.

"There's something going on between those two," she said aloud.

"Huh?" Luke asked as he licked the soft shell of her ear.

"Ethan and Alex. There's something weird happening between them."

Luke pulled her into his arms. "I hope Ethan gets some tonight, because I know I sure as hell am," he said incorrigibly.

Emma laughed. "You're crazy."

"I love you, Mrs. Forrester," he declared solemnly.

"I love *you*, Mr. Forrester," she replied just as seriously.

"I think we need to practice making little Forresters."

"Do you think we need more practice?" she asked, her tone innocent.

He lowered his lips slowly to hers. "You know what they say. Practice makes perfect."

Taming Alex

෩

Chapter One

In a sea of elegantly dressed beautiful people, Ethan had eyes for only one woman. He sipped his drink, unable to take his gaze off Alexandra Sheridan. Brooding, he studied the curve of her hip, the graceful arch of her neck. He followed the luxurious fall of her chestnut hair down the length of her spine. Every smile, every pout of her lush, kissable lips, was designed to bring him to his knees.

From across the room she turned and caught his stare. He didn't bother to avert his eyes. *What's the use?* The air between them sizzled. His body began to respond. His ears buzzed. He ceased to hear the music and the lively party conversation that surrounded him. Everything else faded in the background when she boldly cocked her head and raised her brows.

He allowed himself a small smile and shrugged. *The ball's in your court.*

The luscious red-painted lips parted and exposed even white teeth. Even from this distance he was blindsided by the power of her smile.

His blood simmered, but his hooded eyes hid the answering heat she ignited. Every muscle tightened in anticipation. *What's your next move, Alex?* He didn't have to wait long, watching intently as she glided through the crowd.

Ethan smiled wryly. Temptation was walking towards him wearing a short silk dress that flaunted shapely legs and four-inch stiletto heels that encased narrow, sexy feet. If he had one weakness, it was her, but it wouldn't do to let her know that. It would give her too much of an advantage. He shifted and gripped his drink firmly when she came to a halt in front of him.

"Ethan."

He took a deep breath. Her voice was sinful, like the rest of her. It reminded him of dark nights and long hours of torrid sex.

Alex looked up at him through her long, sooty lashes. "You're not having a good time?"

"Why do you say that?" He smelled her scent, subtle and light. It teased his senses. Made him want to nuzzle that soft spot at the base of her throat and seek out the secret places she misted with perfume.

Her shoulders moved in a careless shrug. "You're hiding in this corner. It's not like you to hide."

"Who says I'm hiding?" He shot her a lazy smile. "I'm enjoying the view." The dress she was wearing was enough to make a man sit up and take notice. It was bold red — silky — and draped over her in a way that fired one's imagination. It certainly fired his.

Those lush red lips curved. "No date tonight?"

The smooth line of her throat drew his gaze, before it slipped lower to her shadowed cleavage. He itched to pull her bodice down and see what was artfully hidden underneath the elegant silk dress. "Keeping tabs on me, Alex?"

Her full lips kissed the crystal wine goblet she held as she sipped her drink. They glistened damply in a siren's smile. A pang of envy consumed him. He wanted to know her taste, wanted to run his tongue over her lips and dampen them himself.

Alex tilted her head. "Maybe like me, you're ready for something new."

His body clenched at her words, followed by a flash of irritation. He was getting damn tired of this cat-and-mouse game. He frowned and threw her a dark look. "What do you want?"

She just grinned and took his glass, placing it on a nearby table along with hers. To his surprise, she pulled him out to the dance floor and glided into his arms. After a moment's hesitation, he pulled her closer and gripped her hips as she swayed sinuously to the slow, jazzy music. It felt good to hold her. The soft brush of her body against his only whetted his appetite. Soon he was steeped in her scent and lost in the feel of her voluptuous curves. He boldly smoothed a hand over her rounded buttocks. No panty line. *What the hell did she have on underneath?*

Somehow they ended up in a secluded corner, hidden by a couple of huge potted plants. A soft hand came up to touch his face. "Kiss me."

He held her steady when she shifted closer to him. Unbelievable. In the middle of his mother's party, in a crowded ballroom, he was sporting a raging hard-on. What's worse, the little minx knew it. Her sexy pouting smile told him so.

"You're asking for trouble." None too gently, he put her from him and headed for the French doors. Once outside, he pulled air into his parched lungs. Seeking solitude, he stalked around the length of the swimming pool to a shadowed corner of the backyard. He jammed his hands deep into his pockets and surveyed the pale reflection of the moonlight on the tranquil water.

The cool evening quickly enveloped him in its embrace. The heady smell of late-blooming flowers was redolent in the thick night air. Perfect for seduction. If he was a superstitious man, he would think nature was conspiring to aid in his downfall.

A great shuddering breath squeezed from his lungs. He'd wanted Alex for years—but she was untouchable, forbidden. It was an implicit rule—don't sleep with your little sister's best friend. Tonight was different. Tonight he was feeling none of the usual reticence. Tonight he wanted to *take*. He was on the verge of falling headlong into her willing arms. *I'm sick of walking around with a fucking hard-on.*

"Are you afraid that once you kiss me you won't be able to stop?" Alex's soft voice floated into the silence, heavy with challenge. He'd been so lost in thought he hadn't even heard her approach.

He slowly turned to face her. "You're playing with fire."

She brushed against him, igniting the flames. "Play with me, Ethan. Let's burn together." She took his hand and placed it on her breast.

He cursed softly. He was no more able to stop himself from curving around the plump mound, than from brushing the turgid tip that pushed insistently against her silk dress. "Go, Alex."

She lifted her chin. "Why won't you admit you want me, too?"

"Take my advice. Leave me," he repeated in a strangled voice.

She stepped closer, trapping his hand between them. "You're a fraud, Ethan. How many times have I caught you looking at me when you thought I didn't notice? Just tonight you couldn't take your eyes off me."

He clenched his jaw tight and didn't answer.

Alex reached up and gave him an openmouthed kiss. He held himself rigid, but could only do it for a few seconds before he allowed his lips to soften against hers. The kiss was slow and full of heat. With her tongue, she skillfully drew him into an erotic dueling game that knocked him off his feet. He was dazed when it ended.

Her sweet breath fanned gently against his lips. "It's only fair to warn you. I don't give up easily." She turned and sashayed the few feet to the pool house. He followed her with his gaze as she opened the door and quietly shut it behind her. Moments later, lights came on in the bungalow and cast distorted shadows on the swimming pool.

His fists clenched. He couldn't go on like this much longer. He needed to take care of this simmering attraction between them. *Simmering?* It was a fucking furnace, ready to explode. She was one hell of a package, sexy as all get out and not afraid to show it.

His eyes locked on the closed door. *What am I going to do with you, Alex?* But deep down inside, he was afraid it was a foregone conclusion. He was a goner, ready to succumb and lose himself in her delicious body.

He froze as the door opened once again. The evening temperature instantly rose several degrees as she appeared on the threshold. One shapely leg was propped up on an antique chair. Ensnared, knowing he shouldn't, but unable to stop himself, he watched eagerly as she rolled down her thigh-high stocking. He greedily devoured every inch of skin she revealed. The other stocking followed the first.

He drew in a shaky breath. Any minute now, somebody was going to come out of the French doors and witness her little striptease. The words he was about to say stuck in his throat when she lowered her dress and pushed it down her hips. His tongue wedged to the roof of his mouth and he couldn't look away as she shimmied seductively out of it.

His teeth snapped together at the sight of her bare breasts. They were more beautiful than he'd imagined, lush and full, tipped with dusky pink areolas. He could only stare as she bent and discarded the flimsy thong she wore.

Alex straightened. Her fingertip brushed against her nipple before coasting down her smooth belly. "I want you here," her fingers disappeared between plump pussy lips, "deep inside me. I want you to fuck me, Ethan. I'm not afraid to admit it."

Her gaze drifted down his front, where his eager cock pushed against his pants unashamedly. "I know you want me, too. What are you going to do about it?" she asked, her voice low and husky. She walked away, leaving the door open in blatant invitation.

Ethan swallowed thickly. *Goddammit.*

Once he accepted her challenge, nothing was going to be the same. But he was only a man—and he'd just reached the point of no return. He stepped towards the pool house.

He was ready to fall.

* * * * *

Alex trembled in front of the dresser mirror. Her heart thudded nervously. She'd never stripped to seduce a man before.

Would it work?

The door behind her closed firmly. Her heart leapt to her throat as Ethan appeared behind her. An air of recklessness surrounded him—he looked dangerous. Sharp tension filled the air.

Her eyes met his in the mirror. "Did you enjoy the show?"

He gave a short, strained laugh as he came closer. "The little striptease? I would have to be made of stone not to enjoy it." He bent and kissed the soft spot where her shoulder and neck met. "What am I going to do with you?"

She'd waited so long for this, there was no backing out now. She turned and faced him, expelling a trembling breath. "Whatever you want."

He rubbed against her and shook his head. "You're too used to men worshiping at your feet."

She arched to his touch. A thousand needles of sensation struck her all at once, sucking her breath away. "I've wanted you for a long time, Ethan."

He licked the soft shell of her ear. "I know."

"You want me, too." In a bold move, she took his hand and placed it within the moist folds of her pussy. Her frustration mounted when he kept stubbornly still.

"You're too used to calling the shots when it comes to men."

Her breath came out shaky. "What's that got to do with us?" Alex pushed his coat off his broad shoulders and let it fall to the floor. The buttons on his snowy white dress shirt were no match for her determined fingers. Soon, the two sides of his shirt gaped open. Her gaze was frankly admiring as she took in the rippled muscles of his torso. His body was strong enough to melt any woman's defenses. He screamed sex, sex, sex. And boy, she wanted lots of it with him.

She slid her hand down his washboard abs to dip briefly in his navel before following the hair that arrowed down and disappeared into his pants. His muscles contracted under her light touch. She loosened his belt buckle, at the same time standing on tiptoe to fasten her lips to his neck.

"Alexandra," he growled warningly.

It was too late to stop. With the button and zipper undone, she pushed the trousers down his thighs. She breathed deeply before she dropped to her knees in front of him and pulled out his heavily engorged cock. Her mouth went dry. He was thick and long with a broad mushroom-shaped head.

"I need to taste you."

He closed his eyes in surrender. A deep thrill slithered down her spine and converged on her pussy. She tongued him quickly, briefly.

The thick head of his cock nudged her lips. "Lick it, Alex."

One slow flick of her tongue tore a muted groan from him. She licked around and around, relaxed and unhurried.

He gritted his teeth. "Suck all of it. No more teasing."

Excitement wound through her bloodstream at his growled order. His voice was raspy, his breathing rough and uneven. Her lips covered the wide head, enveloping him in her mouth. Her tongue stroked and licked and teased. The hungry, choked moan he uttered brought fresh moisture to her pussy. She sucked him slow and deep, lingering over every lick and tight, wet suction. He was delicious. Her hand came up and cupped his testicles, the skin tightening under her light grip. The feel of the baby-soft skin in contrast to the tensile strength of his body tore at her control. Her pulse raced madly. There were so many things she wanted to do to bring him pleasure. Only with Ethan did she feel this out of control, this eager to please. The harsh groan he expelled was music to her ears. She looked up, noting the tight lines of strain around his beautiful lips and felt the powerful tremor that rocked him. A heady feeling of triumph filled her.

"You're gonna make me come," he warned gutturally.

"Hmm." She stretched her lips over him and started all over again, going deeper and faster, intensifying her caresses.

"Damn it, Alex," he moaned desperately before surrendering. All the warning she got was a grunt a mere second before he blasted deep in her mouth. She worked her throat as she enthusiastically swallowed. She gradually relaxed as she licked up the last drop, briefly dipping to lovingly kiss the tight testicles cupped in her palm.

He pulled her up and buried his face in her hair. "God, you're incredible."

She rubbed her breasts against the soft hair on his chest, her nipples puckering tightly. She couldn't stop touching him, running her lips down his neck, his throat, back up to his ear.

"I want to taste every inch of you." He swooped down and took her mouth in a blazingly hot kiss.

Her eyes drifted closed as she clung to him and willingly went along for the ride. He touched her everywhere. She moaned and shuddered. His fingertips feathered down her front and encircled her breasts, going around and around in ever smaller circles until they surrounded the taut tips. Alex arched her back and whimpered a protest. He uttered a strained laugh before he obliged her by brushing against her nipples. It wasn't enough. Her next breath was taken from her as he pulled and squeezed and sent sparks of pleasure shooting through her.

"But I don't think I'll be able to wait that long," he muttered thickly.

"Ethan," she moaned.

His hand slid down the slight swell of her belly before finding the smooth skin of her pussy. He delved into the moist folds and honed in on her clit. A feverish shiver overtook her, her world rocked and trembled. She was as weak as a baby in his arms, parting her legs wider at his muttered order.

It didn't take long for her to come—she was too aroused for that. With a soft cry, she exploded in absolute rapture. Ethan rode out her orgasm, fingers still deep in her body, pulling the last tremor from the very depths of her being. After the dizzying ride was over, she clung to him weakly. He kissed her softly before putting her gently from him and righting his clothes.

"Be at my place tomorrow night at seven." He pressed another brief, hard kiss on her parted lips before walking out the way he came in.

BORDERS

BORDERS
BOOKS AND MUSIC
McCARTHY RANCH MARKETPLACE
15 RANCH DRIVE
MILPITAS CA 95035

```
STORE: 0087   REG: 05/86  TRAN#: 3993
SALE          05/16/2006  EMP:  00049

ORIG STR:0404 REG:02 TR:4387 EMP:00050
CASH      05/14/2006  DO NOT WANT
```

RETURN
JAGGED GIFT

	8390783	QP T	8.62-R
11.49	$2.87 PROMO		
Return	Subtotal		8.62-
		CALIFORNIA 8.25%	.71-R

PURCHASE
INSATIABLE

	8390782	QP T	10.99
Purchase	Subtotal		10.99
		CALIFORNIA 8.25%	.91
1 Item	Total		2.57
	CASH		2.57

05/16/2006 06:41PM

Check our store inventory online
at www.bordersstores.com

Shop online at www.borders.com

BORDERS.

GET a $20 Gift Card:

Get the card that gives you points toward books, music, and movies every time you use it. Call 800.294.0038 to apply for the Borders and Waldenbooks Visa Card and get a $20 Gift Card after your first purchase with the card. For complete details, please visit www.chase.com/applybordersvisa.

Returns to Borders Stores:

Merchandise presented for return, including sale or marked-down items, must be accompanied by the original Borders store receipt. Returns must be completed within 30 days of purchase. The purchase price will be refunded in the medium of purchase (cash, credit card, or gift card). Items purchased by check may be returned for cash after 10 business days.

Merchandise unaccompanied by the original Borders store receipt, or presented for return beyond 30 days from date of purchase, must be carried by Borders at the time of the return. The lowest price offered for the item during the 12-month period prior to the return will be refunded via a gift card.

Opened videos, discs, and cassettes may only be exchanged for replacement copies of the original item.

Periodicals, newspapers, and out-of-print, collectible and pre-owned items may not be returned.

Returned merchandise must be in saleable condition.

T-Mobile HotSpot

Borders is a T-Mobile HotSpot. Enjoy wireless broadband Internet service for your laptop or PDA

Alex slumped on the chair. *That was it?* Seething with frustration, she stared at the closed door. The night was supposed to end differently. Visions of sweat-slicked bodies writhing on tangled sheets filled her mind. That was how she wanted to spend the night with Ethan. The taste she'd had of him was all too brief. She wanted more. A whole lot more. She needed to fuck him.

Tomorrow night couldn't come soon enough.

Chapter Two

Alex walked into her apartment, arms laden with gaily colored shopping bags. Giddy with excitement, she tossed them down on her bed and pulled out the dress she'd bought for her date with Ethan tonight. A dress designed to knock his socks off. *Along with anything else he's wearing.* She grinned. The dress was a heavenly blue creation that whispered and flowed with every movement. All it had taken was one look and Alex fell in love. It was outrageously expensive and took a big chunk out of her savings, but what the hell. She held the dress up in front of the mirror. It was deceptively simple, yet sexy. Perfect.

She tossed the dress on the bed and looked at her reflection critically. The full-length mirror was honest and unforgiving. Her body was not the slim, svelte kind. In her opinion she was *too* curvy. Those ten extra pounds she couldn't lose seemed to have found a permanent home in her hips. She made a face. Nothing she could do about that. Her breasts were probably the best part of her body. They were on the large side, but seemed to balance out her rounded hips. She examined her legs. They weren't half bad.

With a careless shrug, she turned away from the mirror and walked to the kitchen. Picking up the mail from the tiled counter, she flipped through the pile. At the bottom was a thick, cream-colored envelope. Her stomach sank. With an all-too-familiar feeling of dread, she tore the missive open and pulled out the elegantly embossed contents. It was an invitation to her mother's seventh wedding.

Her lips twisted. So husband number six hadn't worked out after all. What else was new? It sure didn't take Margaret Sheridan-McKinley-and-a-slew-of-other-names long to find victim number seven. Alex eyed the costly paper used for the invitation. Why did her Mom even bother? She had no intention of being a party to her mother's insane need to marry every man she dated. It made a mockery of the institution of marriage.

With a heavy sigh, she tossed the invitation back on the counter and trudged to the shower. Long ago she had decided that marriage was not for her. Love was a temporary feeling, and commitment was something very few people could live up to. Just look at her Mom. She was the perfect example that showed getting married didn't mean a damn thing anymore.

Thick steam slowly filled the bathroom. Her thoughts churned painfully, dominated by bitter memories. Her gaze followed the water as it sluiced down her body before continuing down the drain. *I wish I could get rid of my troubles that way.* She raised her face to the gentle massage of the shower. If only it were that easy.

* * * * *

The taxi dropped her off in front of the Upper East Side townhouse Ethan called home. Her knees shook so badly she almost tripped on the ridiculously high heels she wore. A nervous laugh made its way out of her trembling lips. Butterflies flitted around her stomach frantically and her hands were cold and damp. She navigated the steps up to the front door and moved to press the doorbell. The door opened abruptly and Ethan stood on the threshold. Alex swallowed at the sight of him in a dark blue shirt that brought out the color of his eyes. He looked delicious.

He was just as busy devouring her, his murmured greeting washing over her. Heat began to claw its way up her insides. *Would it be a terrible faux pas if she pulled off her clothes and just asked him to fuck her right here?* She blushed at the thought. In the next second, her mind went blank as he bent and gave her a slow, toe-curling kiss. When next she was aware, he had pulled her inside.

His eyes gleamed sexily. "Hi."

Warmth flooded her insides at the intimacy in his tone. "Hi."

His hands splayed on her back, restlessly roving up and down. A short tug brought her up close to him. "You look beautiful."

The heat emanating from him threatened to burn right through her dress. Her breath caught in her throat as she brushed against the erection he sported. "You don't look so bad yourself."

He swooped down and gave her several short, teasing kisses. Their lips touched and parted over and over. Heat pooled in her pussy. Her nipples pushed insistently against the silk of her dress, the soft material rasping deliciously against the taut tips.

"Are you hungry?" he asked, his breath fanning the soft skin of her neck.

She laughed huskily. "Not for food."

His lips opened over hers and their tongues tangled. Alex began to burn. Not a slow burn, but a firestorm that suddenly broke and raged. Ethan was unstoppable, a driving force that pushed through and completely overtook her. Her zipper loosened. With a little help from him, her dress fell in a puddle at her feet. Her unfettered breasts fell into his hands, their distended tips pushing hard against his palms.

Alex whimpered in need, busy unbuttoning his shirt. He backed her against a wall and impatiently pushed her hands aside, tugging his shirt open, uncaring that buttons went flying in all directions. Drugged by his kisses, she rubbed against him, her nipples two tight points that burrowed amid the soft body hair on his chest.

"Let's get rid of this," he muttered impatiently. One sharp tug was all it took to tear the flimsy thong away from her hips.

Her legs rubbed restlessly together, falling open to admit one hard male thigh in between. His knee slid between hers, the faint rasping feel of his trousers against her inner thigh driving her crazy. He gripped her tightly and lifted until her breasts were level with his mouth. A long moan was ripped from her as he mouthed the sensitive tips. She held him to her and desperately tried to push more of her flesh against him.

"You taste so good, Alex." His voice was rough, guttural.

"Ethan," she gasped desperately, feeling herself burn hotter and hotter.

"I'm right here," he assured her. He bent and suckled the soft skin of her neck, his hands curving around her ass.

Alex fought to relax, fought to breathe and stay standing. She clung to him tightly, moaning desperately at the brief swipe he gave her sopping pussy. In the next second, she was whimpering incoherently as his fingers plunged inside. Her hips arched to his touch, ripples of heat penetrating her womb.

She climbed higher, and knew she wasn't going to last. His dark head was pillowed against her chest. All she could focus on was his lips, his hands, and oh God, his tongue. He was driving her insane. "I need to—" she grabbed his belt and pulled it from the loops, "—help me, Ethan!"

He finished the job himself, pushing down his trousers. His erect cock nudged the lips of her pussy. "I'm sorry," he muttered, breathing heavily. He hitched her legs higher around his waist. "I'll make it up to you next time," was all he said before his cock pushed through her channel and slid home.

Her breath shuddered. Alex closed her eyes and wrapped her arms tightly around his neck. He filled every inch and took what was offered with no apologies. It was rough and primal. *And it was oh so good*, she thought dizzily.

The tender tissues of her pussy were assaulted by the unforgiving rhythm he adopted. "Fuck me," she whispered in his ear. "Don't ever stop."

A violent tremor rocked her. He thrust deeper, the primitive animal in him taking over. She wasn't any better, moaning and pleading with him to continue. Sweat slicked his back, her hands sliding against the hot skin. Her legs locked tight around him as he stroked deep inside her moist depths.

Alex screamed as pleasure exploded inside her—she contracted wildly around his cock. He gripped her hips and held her still as he let out a rough groan and followed her over. Hot seed splashed the clenching walls of her pussy as she greedily absorbed every tremor that shook her body. She panted, waiting for her pulse to go back to normal. The sound of his heavy breathing washed over her. Her lips curved. She wasn't the only one who was thoroughly shaken up.

Ethan slid his hands under her legs, hooking them firmly around his waist before heading up the winding staircase. Alex hung on, wide-eyed and flushed with embarrassment.

"Put me down, Ethan," she mumbled against his neck. "I'm too heavy to carry up the stairs."

"Shut up," he replied in an affectionate tone.

The ascent was pure torment as his still-lodged cock shifted and thrust in her as he took the stairs one step at a time. Unbelievably, a kernel of arousal grew and blossomed inside her once more. Her pussy clenched rhythmically. He thickened inside her, growing long and hard during the final steps up the stairs. There was no stopping the low moan that erupted from between her lips. One look at him and she knew he was in as deep as she was. Tightening her hold on him, she lifted up and down, eyes closing at the sheer pleasure of impaling herself on him.

"You're killing me" he gritted out as he kicked his bedroom door open.

Her gaze was glued to his lips, dazed and consumed by the hunger to possess them. She ran her tongue around and around the firm curves of his upper and lower lip, quickly slipping in between to graze his teeth. She gasped at the large hand that curved around her nape and pulled her hair back, tipping her face up.

"You're so beautiful, Alex." His gaze grew hooded, his blue eyes unfathomable. "I want to slow down and make love to you properly, but I don't know if I have the patience to do that." He licked the side of her neck. "I want to taste you, memorize every inch and every curve."

"Ethan," she whimpered. He took her lips in a kiss that devoured, stoked and soothed. Too late—she was already on fire.

He gently deposited her on the bed, slipping out of her pussy. His cock glistened damply with their combined juices as it rose between them. A soft moan of protest slipped from her lips, feeling bereft without him inside her. Ethan ignored that, trailing his fingers down to her breasts. He squeezed them gently, pushing the mounds together. "These have driven me crazy. I could suck your nipples for hours." He dipped and pulled a distended tip deep in his mouth, his cheeks hollowing as he suckled.

She tunneled her fingers through his hair and sought to get closer. In one swift stroke, he pushed inside her pussy once more. He drew in a shaky breath and held still.

"Oh," she cried out helplessly. "I can feel you so deep, Ethan."

He gave a small grin before he sat back on his haunches, draping her legs over his. It was the most beautiful thing in the world to have him openly admire her. His intense blue eyes raked over her. Alex writhed on the bed, mutely begging him to move.

"Touch your breasts," he muttered hoarsely.

More than willing to play his game, she cupped the full weight of the heavy mounds in her hands and rotated her palms against the taut tips. His eyes glinted hotly. He gave her two deep strokes that brought a moan to her lips. He palmed her ass and squeezed.

Alex drew in a huge shuddering breath. Blunt-tipped fingers rubbed suggestively against the puckered rosebud between her cheeks. "Ethan?" Desire mixed with apprehension filled that one word.

"I want to fuck you here," he whispered gutturally. "I want to watch my cock go deep in your ass and fuck you out of your mind."

Just like that, she came. The words he uttered sounded unbelievably sexy, so forbidden that she just toppled over. Dimly, she heard his strangled groan above her as he pounded into her. He went deep again and again until he came with one great thrust. She trembled, caught in a maelstrom of pleasure so intense it was painful. Feeling as weak and helpless as a baby, she didn't protest as he settled down next to her and pulled her close.

Closing her eyes, she snuggled against his warmth with a satisfied smile on her lips.

Chapter Three

Alex walked into the Cup o' Java and headed directly to the small table tucked in the back of the coffee shop. Saturday brunch was a tradition for her and Emma, something they'd done faithfully for years. Now it was every other Saturday since Emma's marriage. Her lips twitched. Luke was very possessive of his wife's time.

"It's about time you got here," Emma began in a teasing tone. "I was beginning to think you weren't going to show."

"Sorry," she muttered. "I overslept."

Interest glowed in her best friend's eyes. "Hmm. Do tell."

Alex didn't answer as the waitress came with two steaming cups of coffee and took their order before leaving. Emma looked at her expectantly. "Well? Who was the date?"

She used the excuse of sipping her coffee to delay answering. But Emma wasn't about to be deterred. "You're stalling, Alex. Do I know this guy?"

She choked. The coffee really was too hot.

Emma's eyes narrowed shrewdly. "That's it, isn't it? I know this guy. That's why you're being so secretive."

Alex hid her troubled gaze behind lowered eyelashes. She'd left Ethan in the wee hours of the morning. He'd been asleep on his stomach, the thin sheet low over his hips and a muscular arm stretched out on his side. He'd expected her to stay, that much she knew. But she'd never stayed overnight with anybody. Ever. It smacked too much of a willingness to commit and raised too many expectations.

She sighed. She'd no doubt deal with him later.

A frown furrowed the smooth skin on Emma's forehead. "This isn't like you, Alex. You're usually more forthcoming than this." She leaned forward. "Is everything all right?"

Alex winced inwardly. *Everything's peachy. Oh and by the way, I just slept with your brother.* "Of course. I'm just a little tired, that's all."

Emma was about to say something but stopped when she glanced behind Alex. Her eyes widened with surprise then she grinned with delight. "Well, hello. I thought you had an early golf game today."

Luke bent down to kiss his wife on the lips. "That's what I thought, too. Imagine my surprise when Ethan showed up on our doorstep this morning."

At the mention of Ethan's name, Alex stiffened. Her stomach sank with dread. *Please, please don't let him be here.*

Luke sat down next to his wife and gave Alex an enigmatic grin. "Hey, Alex."

Alex forced herself to give him a small smile. "Luke."

Emma focused her gaze behind Alex. "Ethan, are you just going to stand there or are you going to join us?"

Oh no.

A masculine hand pulled out the chair next to her. "Hello, Alex."

With reluctance, she turned to him. "Good morning," she replied politely. She couldn't decipher the expression in his eyes. There was an air of brooding calm about him. What was he doing here?

Emma's gaze held a touch of curiosity. The sudden tension in the air was noticeable. "Well, this is nice, us having brunch together."

Ethan hooked an arm casually on Alex's chair. "I actually had other plans. But when I woke up this morning, everything changed."

Alex sat stiffly, unmoving. He obviously wasn't pleased, that much she could tell. She hoped he wouldn't say anything about what had happened last night. She had no wish to air their private issues in front of Emma and Luke.

"Oh," Emma said with a nod. "It worked out for the better then. I can't remember the last time the four of us have been together like this."

Luke ran a hand down his wife's cheek. "You've been rather busy lately, honey." He grinned. "With me."

A light blush spread across Emma's cheeks as she looked at Luke with clear adoration. "Yes, I have, haven't I?"

They fell silent as the waitress brought over two more cups of coffee. Alex used this chance to take a deep breath and compose herself. It was no use letting Ethan see how rattled she was that he was here. She took a sip of her rapidly cooling coffee.

"So, Alex," Ethan began in a conversational tone. "Why did you sneak out last night?"

Alex gasped and almost choked. Her hand shook so badly she had to put the cup back on the table quickly. She swallowed and caught Emma's look of open-mouthed surprise. Luke sat back with a half-grin. *The rat.* He already knew. When she finally turned to Ethan, it was to see him looking back at her, casual as you please, as if he hadn't just dropped a bombshell in front of his sister.

Well, she could give as well as he could. She raised an eyebrow and countered in a tart voice, "You were sleeping like a baby. I didn't want to wake you up."

Emma blinked and looked back and forth between her brother and her best friend. There were a thousand questions in her eyes but Luke stood up and pulled her along. "Come on, honey. Let's go."

She stood up reluctantly. "But—"

Luke wasn't to be deterred. "I think it's best if we leave them to it," he said quietly but firmly. "Besides you need to take care of your husband," he added teasingly.

Emma relented. "I thought I just did that this morning." She turned to Alex, her tone serious, "We have to talk."

Alex gave a tight nod and watched as Luke and Emma walked away. As soon as they were out of earshot, she turned to Ethan furiously. "How could you do that? Why did you have to let them know about us?"

He crossed his arms and gazed back at her calmly. "Why not?"

"Why not?" she repeated. "Because things could get unpleasant after…after," she trailed off.

Ethan raised his eyebrows, waiting for her to continue.

"After we—" she began, then took a deep breath before continuing, "after *this* is over."

"I'm not even close to being done with you, Alexandra," he countered softly. "Not by a long shot."

She flushed. "I just thought we could keep this between us. Emma's my best friend, and you and I will still cross paths in the future."

Ethan leaned forward and stuck his face close to hers. "What made you think I'd want to hide the fact that we're sleeping together?" He snorted in disdain, his eyes blazing hotly. Alex glimpsed the anger he was holding in.

"You always spend the holidays with my family, Alex. Did you think I was going to let my mother put us in different rooms at Thanksgiving or Christmas?" He shook his head. "I'll make sure she puts us in the same room. And I'll make you scream so loud while I fuck you that there won't be any doubt in anybody's mind what we're doing."

Alex glared at him even as the heat his words generated started spreading through her susceptible body. "I just thought we could be discreet about this."

"I'm not about to sneak around like some kid," he declared with barely leashed anger. "We're both adults and if we choose to sleep with each other, then it's nobody's fucking business but ours. Now come here and give me the good morning kiss you cheated me out of."

She exhaled loudly. She was still pissed. "I don't think—"

"Come here. *Now*."

With a resentful huff, she scooted her chair closer. "This really is not—"

Ethan curved a hand around her nape and pulled. He captured her lips in a kiss so hot it curled her toes and effectively shut her up. It took mere seconds before she was lost in the driving possession of his lips and tongue as it tangled with her own. She was dazed when he finally let her up for air.

"I don't care who knows that we're sleeping together," he muttered against her lips. "I want everybody to know that I'm fucking you every day, every night and all the hours in between."

Alex gulped.

"I'm not going to hide, Alex," he finished softly.

She uttered a defeated sigh. "I don't want to, either. I just wanted to avoid any awkwardness when—when this is over," she added lamely.

He gazed into her eyes for long moments before he released an exasperated sigh. "You think too much." He stood up and tossed some bills on the table before threading his fingers with hers. "Let's go."

Alex grabbed her purse. "Where are we going?"

Ethan grinned, looking more relaxed. "We're going on a date."

* * * * *

They spent the entire day together. She was surprised at how at ease she felt with him. There were no uncomfortable lapses in conversation, and she didn't have to work hard to think of something to talk about. It just felt…right to be with him.

What's more, she didn't get the usual feelings of impatience and boredom she felt with other men. Too often, she discovered that out of bed, some guys just weren't interesting at all. Ethan was funny and sexy. He seemed to know instinctively what she liked. It was uncanny at times how well he knew her—but that was hardly surprising. After all, they'd known each other for a long time.

She also discovered what a tactile person he was. He was always touching her, either at the small of her back, the curve of her waist, or merely by linking his fingers with hers. This was all new territory to her. She'd never been touchy-feely with other boyfriends. She never wanted to be the clingy type. But she loved touching Ethan.

The day flew by without her noticing it. That was another thing. She'd *never* spent an entire day with previous boyfriends. Too much togetherness was anathema to her. What had happened to her rule of always keeping it casual? Nothing serious, that was her motto. Commitment was something she just wasn't into. This thing with Ethan wasn't any different, right? *We're just two consenting adults enjoying a sexual affair*, she insisted to herself. Besides, Ethan just wasn't the type to settle down. She'd seen too many women come and go in his life over the years to believe that he would settle down any time soon. When they broke up—and she was sure they eventually would—then she'd just accept it and go on. She'd get over him...wouldn't she? *Just enjoy this time with him, for as long as it lasts.* Somehow the thought didn't sit well with her no matter how she tried to convince herself. She pushed it aside as she followed Ethan into his kitchen for some dinner.

It was a revelation to her how easily he moved around the kitchen as he made the spaghetti sauce and put pasta in the boiling water. With her chin propped in her hand, she followed him with her eyes. *He's so gorgeous.* The top button of his jeans was casually undone and his chest was bare. His body was buff but lean, his deeply tanned skin stretched smoothed over rippled and corded muscles. *And that ass...* The jeans, softened from numerous washings, clung faithfully to his firm backside.

He caught a glimpse of her grin. "What's so funny?"

"I was just thinking you would sell a ton of those jeans if you just posed shirtless in an ad," she said impishly.

"No thanks." He shot her a heated stare. "You look better than I ever did in that shirt, though."

She hid a smile, oddly pleased by his compliment. "I didn't know you could cook."

"I figured I'd do the cooking tonight," he answered dryly. "I haven't forgotten your attempt at lasagna."

Alex flushed and socked him in the arm as he passed by. "Ow," he exclaimed. He couldn't quite mask his teasing grin.

"That's what you get for bringing that up," she sniffed.

He laughed. "How could I forget? The lasagna was so hard it tasted like Italian cardboard."

She picked up a couple of wineglasses and stomped over to the table. "So cooking is not one of my strong suits."

Ethan pulled her into his arms and nuzzled her neck. "We can order in, I don't care. As long as I can have you naked in my bed every night, I'll be fine."

Now what did he mean by that? He was talking as if he wanted a long-term relationship. Probably just a slip of the tongue, she reassured herself. Her attention was diverted by the hard cock brushing against her ass. "We'd better eat before we get sidetracked," she finished faintly.

He laid out bowls of spaghetti on the table before wiggling his eyebrows suggestively. "I agree. We need to keep up our strength."

When Ethan was in a teasing mood, he was damn near irresistible. He wasn't a bad cook, either. The spaghetti was delicious. She hid a small smile at the way he kept touching her. Long fingers smoothed down her arm before grazing her thigh. The constant sensation kept her simmering.

"Spend the night with me," he invited huskily. "The whole night, Alex. No sneaking out."

Alex bit her lip and tried to explain. "Ethan, I'm not in the habit of spending the night—with anyone. I've always been that way."

His eyes darkened. "I'm glad to hear it."

Her gaze slid away. "Please understand."

"I want to sleep with you in my arms. I want to wake up with you beside me." He nuzzled her neck. "Hmm?"

Her heart melted. She wanted that too. But she'd always held steadfast to her rule of not staying the entire night. The words "long-term" and "commitment" kept flashing in her mind. It would be easier to bounce back and escape unhurt if she kept a certain distance in the first place.

Ethan sucked the soft skin on her neck. "I don't snore. And I promise not to hog the entire bed."

She uttered a reluctant chuckle. What was the harm, just this once? Would it be too bad to actually *sleep* with him? Damn it, she was softening and she knew he knew it. His hands roamed up and down her back, ending by cupping her ass and pulling her up against him. Her eyes drifted closed. It really was a no-brainer when he was touching her like this. How could she say no? Ignoring the little voice inside her mind that whispered *don't do it*, she finally nodded. "Okay."

The gleam in his eyes was thoroughly male and sexual. Anticipation skittered down her spine. Sex. It hung thickly in the air and turned the atmosphere several degrees hotter.

A large, masculine hand found its way under her shirt. "Eat up, Alex. I've got *big* plans for you."

* * * * *

Dappled morning sunlight brought out the rich highlights in her chestnut hair. He'd been unable to take his gaze off her since she came down the stairs. He breathed deeply, slowly sipping his coffee. Breakfast with Alex was cozy and intimate, the silence companionable. Contentment settled on his shoulders. He could very easily get used to having her around.

Absently rubbing the soles of her feet as they perched on his lap, he studied her thoughtfully. She spread cream cheese on her bagel and chewed slowly, her eyes on the newspaper. Her hair was pinned haphazardly on top of her head, long shiny strands brushing her cheeks. Even without makeup, her skin was clear and smooth. She had never looked more beautiful to him than right now.

As a rule, he never invited a woman to stay overnight. Too often, it resulted in misunderstandings and expectations. He'd also come to realize long ago that he couldn't stand the nonstop chatter women seemed to find necessary. Alex was different. She was just as content to read the paper with him, not filling the silence with meaningless conversation. They'd always gotten along.

He remembered the time they got stuck in a snowstorm in his family's cabin up in the mountains. He smiled at the memory. Everybody else had gone into town to take in a movie. Alex had pleaded a headache and stayed behind. He'd found himself making up an excuse to remain in the cabin. To keep her company? Maybe. He couldn't remember. A blizzard had suddenly blown in, trapping them inside the cabin for two whole days. He realized now he'd had far more fun then than he dared admit. They'd played Monopoly. He grinned. Alex had a strong competitive streak in her. Before he knew it, she'd bought most of the properties and he'd had to pay her exorbitant rent every time he landed on any of them.

He'd beat her soundly in chess. She'd trounced him in three games of pool. She absolutely had no talent for poker but she was hell-on-wheels with blackjack. She also had a wicked sense of humor and made him laugh until they were both rolling on the floor.

They were compatible on so many levels.

Even then, he'd noticed the tempting curve of her wide lips. He'd caught himself looking at the long, lustrous length of her hair, wanting to reach out and touch it. He knew someday those plump girlish curves would be voluptuous as hell. But she was *Alex*, Emma's best friend. She was like his little sister, for God's sake. She was around so much—she was like a member of the family.

When the weather had cleared, he'd even let her drive his most prized possession, a little English sports car. She roared into town, proudly showing off her newly acquired driving skills. He laughed and bought her ice cream, only to witness her broken heart when she caught her boyfriend in the ice cream parlor with another girl. He took her home, letting her cry it out. He didn't tell her about going back to see the lying son of a bitch later and teaching him a lesson he would never forget.

"Stay away from her," he warned in a coldly furious voice.

The jackass wiped the blood from his lip. "What do you care? What's a college boy like you doing with a high school chick like her, anyway? Is she giving you some? Don't tell me you like her," he sneered.

Ethan had broken the boy's nose. He'd never resorted to violence before. Somehow seeing the hurt and tears in Alex's eyes had triggered something in him. Stunned, he'd driven home, pulling into a deserted parking lot along the way. The words the boy had thrown at him brought a prickling of unease to his mind. *Was it true? Did he like her in that way?* At the time, he'd dismissed the thought. He'd concluded he just felt overprotective, much like an older brother would.

Had he been kidding himself, even then?

Pulling himself back into the present, his gaze was once again drawn to her mouth. For as long as he'd known her, Alex'd had an adorable habit of nipping the soft curve of her lower lip. In that instant, he felt a curious tug deep in his heart, a feeling completely unfamiliar to him.

Was he falling in love with her?

He stilled. The boy's words came back to haunt him. Had it started then, when he'd seen the stricken look on her face and just wanted to wipe it all away? Was that when he'd started feeling differently about her? Maybe. He didn't know. Couldn't tell. Had he always felt this way but been unwilling to face it? A dozen questions flitted through his mind, questions he didn't know the answers to. The only thing he *was* sure of was that he felt deeply about her.

Out of bed, he felt at ease with her. In bed, she set him on fire. Alex was the perfect woman for him. His lips twisted wryly. It had to be one of life's greatest ironies that he was falling for the commitment-phobic Alexandra Sheridan.

She chose that moment to look up and throw him a puzzled smile. "What?" she asked, wiping playfully at her face. "Do I have cream cheese on my face?"

As he sat there grappling with his newfound feelings, he watched her smile fade uncertainly. Something indefinable and intense hung over them, turning the atmosphere thick and heavy.

"What's wrong?" she repeated faintly.

"Come here," he commanded gruffly. He pulled her onto his lap, arranging her thighs over his. It was easy enough to unzip his jeans and pull out his cock. Her breathing grew shaky and uneven.

His cock slipped inside her in slow degrees. Ethan clamped his jaw. "You're so tight."

She moaned softly.

His heart thudded loudly in time with hers. "Take your top off, Alex."

As fast as lightning, she whipped the shirt over her head. He bent and pulled a distended nipple into his mouth. All rational thought threatened to fly out the window at the sensation of being inside her again. Control. He needed to slow it down and control the pace. A slight shifting of her hips made him grip her tight and steady. She whispered her protest.

"Ethan, *please*."

His eyes flashed a very hot, very male look. "Tell me you need me." He moved just enough for her to throw her head back in ecstasy. "Say it, Alex. Say you need me to fuck you now."

A shuddering breath escaped her.

His tongue went around and around the taut nipple, circling but not quite touching the aching tip. "I'm waiting."

Alex cupped his face in her hands and looked directly into his eyes. "I n-need you to fuck me now."

"There's nothing wrong with saying you need me." He thrust deeply, slowly. "See what you get in return?"

"I want more, Ethan. Harder please."

Whatever control he had broke at that point. "Ride me, Alex. Fast and hard." He braced his legs as she began to ride him furiously. He was breathing hard, his pulse jumping crazily. Every stroke took him deeper, drove him higher. His fingers bit into the delicate skin of her hips as the sexy mewling noises she made consumed him. The ride was fast and furious.

Dimly, he heard her breathless cry as she shuddered. Her orgasm triggered his, pleasure shooting from the base of his spine. He sought to surround her with his warmth and fill her with his essence, to make her feel what he was feeling. The tiny kisses he rained on her shoulder soothed her, gradually helping her relax.

"Move in with me."

Alex froze in his arms. "What did you say?"

He tenderly pushed her damp hair aside. "You heard me," was his gentle answer.

The atmosphere between them noticeably cooled. Wordlessly, she pushed out of his arms and pulled on her discarded shirt. "I can't do that, Ethan."

His jaw tightened. "Why not?"

Jade eyes flashed at him in anger. "It's crazy, that's why. We've only spent one night together and already you want me to move in?"

"We've known each other for a long time," he argued, barely keeping his temper in check.

"That doesn't mean anything," she replied flatly.

"It does to me." He eyed her stiff back, noting the angry set of her shoulders and the muscles she held so tightly. "I have never invited a woman to spend the night with me Alex, much less move in. It's not a commitment I take lightly."

She winced. "It's too soon."

Too late he realized his mistake in using the "c" word. *Fuck, it's too late to take it back now.* "Too soon?" he repeated harshly. "I've been through enough relationships to see that this is different. I'm not just jumping blindly here." He dared her to disagree. "You know me better than that."

Her lips thinned and she stubbornly remained silent.

Unable to help himself, he moved closer to her. "We have something special. I knew it from the first moment I took you into my arms. I tried hard to resist you." He gave a self-deprecating laugh. "It was a losing battle. Why do you think I tried so hard to ignore you? I knew once we got together, it would be unlike any relationship you or I had before. I just *knew* it deep inside." He willed her to see his point. "We've known each other too long, Alex. We know each other too well for this to be just a sexual affair. I'm willing to see where it takes us." He tipped her chin up. "Are you?"

Alex spun around, dislodging his hand. "You don't understand."

He doggedly followed her, turning her around to face him. "On the contrary, I understand you very well." He was determined to keep his voice calm and steady. "I know how you operate. How many times have I seen you run away at the first sign of serious involvement? You shy away from commitment. The poor fools didn't know what they were getting into." His eyes grew somber. "I do."

He breathed deeply to ease the tightness of his chest. "This is all new for me, too. I've never wanted anybody the way I want you." He curved his hand around her nape, rubbing her soft skin in an attempt to maintain some kind of closeness with her. "I want to spend Saturday afternoons with you and then have leisurely Sunday breakfasts together." The image brought a smile to his lips. "Don't you want to see where this might lead? Take this chance with me, Alex. A leap of faith, hmm?"

A fat tear rolled down her cheek. "It's just the sex."

Ethan snorted gently. "Credit me with some sense. I can pick up the phone and have a willing woman here in an hour," he said bluntly. He strove to make her understand, he *needed* to make her see the truth in his words. "We have something special. Don't throw it away."

"Why can't we just have sex like other people?" she cried in frustration.

His nostrils flared. *She was so damn stubborn.* "I don't want an affair. I want a committed relationship with you."

She bit her lip. "That's something I can't give you."

His reply was short, succinct and had her wincing. "It's all or nothing, Alex."

Shoulders stiff, she turned and walked away.

"You're scared of commitment, I know that." His words stopped her mid-stride. "I'm willing to wait while you deal with that. I need you to face your fear so you'll be free and clear when you come back to me." He deliberately infused his voice with confidence. "I'll be waiting."

Without speaking, she turned and faced him. Her beautiful jade eyes were dull with misery. He steeled himself against the sight. "I will not play games with you, Alex. This is between you and me. *We* will work this out." His lips firmed. "No other person will be involved." At her faintly puzzled look, he continued. "I'll give you time, but you have to play by the rules." He held her eyes to emphasize his point. "I don't share."

She whirled and left the kitchen. He raised his eyes heavenward and hoped she'd look at the mussed sheets on the bed and remember every single, mind-destroying erotic thing they'd done to each other last night.

He stood silently by the stairs when Alex came down, his face carefully devoid of any emotion. Her steps were heavy as she stepped out the front door, not bothering to look at him. His heart sank. It was only by sheer force of will that he managed not to go after her and make her listen. He would give her space, for a limited time, to resolve her personal issues. This was something she needed to do on her own.

Chapter Four

Alex kicked the thick blankets aside, her legs rubbing restlessly against the soft sheets on the bed. Barely five minutes had passed since she'd last checked the time. It was close to midnight, and she wasn't feeling the least bit sleepy. Her mind was churning with thoughts of Ethan.

Since walking out on him a few days ago her nights had been sheer torture. Plagued by insomnia, she'd tossed and turned every night. Alex plumped a pillow and hugged it tightly. Blood was pumping heavily through her veins and her breasts ached with tightly puckered tips. Her skin was sensitive to the slightest touch. Like an addict, her body was looking for a fix — a fix that only one man could give her.

She eyed the phone longingly. *Should she call him?* How long could she last like this? She turned away only to look back a second later. Before she could change her mind, she picked it up and punched his number. Ethan answered on the second ring.

"I can't sleep," she said without preliminaries. Her voice throbbed huskily with longing.

"Me either."

Alex imagined him lying on his bed wearing absolutely nothing, the sheets resting provocatively low on his hips. Her sigh whispered over the phone.

"I could be there in a few minutes, Alex." His deep voice was sinfully tempting. "You're hungry."

She moaned softly in agreement.

"All you have to do is tell me what I want to hear." The sexy tone was persuasive, cajoling. "Tell me and you won't have to suffer sleepless nights, craving the satisfaction only I can give you."

"You want me as much as I want you." She dared him to deny it.

"I do." There was no hesitation in his answer. It was clear and direct.

Alex was bordering on desperation. She needed to sway him from this ridiculous notion of commitment. Her voice lowered seductively. "I'm touching my breasts, pretending it's you, Ethan. Squeezing and tugging my nipples. Your touch is rough, yet gentle as you fuck me."

The deep breath he released echoed loudly in her ear. "Do you know what I did last night, Alex? I got myself off thinking of you. I pictured you lying on my bed, naked and waiting for me. I imagined your pussy, moist and glistening, open and begging for my touch."

It was her turn to inhale sharply, little points of pleasure attacking her sensitive skin. Her pulse rate accelerated.

"It wasn't enough," he said flatly. "I need the real thing. I need you just like you need me."

Arousal fed her frustration. "The real thing is right here. You can have me anytime."

When he spoke, his voice had more than a hint of frustration, too. "Tell me what I want to hear, and I'll fuck you long and hard, in every possible way." There was steely determination underlying his words. "But until then, we'll just have to suffer nights like this."

She bit back an angry retort and sought to get even instead. She allowed the longing and need she felt to surface in her voice as she pushed her fingers deep inside her body. "I'm pretending it's your fingers inside my pussy, Ethan." A moan wound its way from between her parted lips, her breaths coming faster. "It feels so good, oh God." Her eyes drifted shut as she sought her clit and massaged it softly. Already slick and wet with arousal, her fingers slid smoothly inside her passage. She panted and dimly heard him expel a shaky breath. Too hungry and too long denied satisfaction, she came quickly. Shudders overtook her body and she whimpered in the back of her throat. The silence over the line was telling. Alex gripped the phone tightly. "That's what you're missing."

With that, she hung up on him. A great yawning emptiness took over and quickly dimmed the pleasure she'd received from her orgasm. It was temporary and hardly enough. She pressed the heel of her hands against her closed eyes. Though she hated to admit it, Ethan was right about one thing. She needed the flesh and blood man inside her, nothing else would do. Only Ethan could put her out of misery.

* * * * *

One hellish week had passed since she'd walked out on him. She had done nothing but toss and turn every night, lying awake until the wee hours of the morning. As a result, she was tired, irritable and unable to focus on work. In a vain attempt to get Ethan out of her mind, she agreed to go out with a man she didn't even like.

"Is something wrong with your food, Alex?"

She blinked. Whatever had possessed her to go out to dinner with Matt Rayburn anyway? Oh sure, he was attractive, if one liked the bulky, muscular, bodybuilding type. She didn't.

A small smile parted her lips. "The food's fine, Matt. I don't mean to be rude, but my mind is on work." *Liar.*

He nodded in agreement. "You work too hard. What you need is a man who will take care of you so you won't ever need to work another day in your life."

She frowned. *What kind of a life is that?* Matt Rayburn owned a string of highly successful gyms and was obviously a rich man. He'd pulled out all the stops to impress her. The restaurant was exclusive and intimate and he'd ordered in flawless French. It wasn't his fault her mind was on a certain tall, dark-haired, blue-eyed stubborn man who made her shiver with just one heated look.

Matt leaned forward. "You look beautiful."

Alex bit back a sigh and discreetly checked her slim watch. *Has it only been an hour?* "Thanks."

He covered her hand on top of the table. "I'm glad you're here with me tonight."

Her response was lost as her gaze was drawn near the front of the restaurant. The maître d' was leading the way for a cool, willowy blonde and her date. Her eyes narrowed in recognition. *Ethan.* What the hell?

Ethan's gaze was inscrutable as he looked at her and Matt, touching briefly on the hand that still covered hers. For a moment, she thought she saw a flicker of anger flash in the deep blue of his eyes but it was gone too quickly. In answer, her eyebrow rose as she looked at him and his companion.

Annoyance shadowed her expression. *He certainly moved on fast.* Her spirits sank further when she saw they were seated only a couple of tables away. Ethan calmly looked back at her. *What did she expect anyway?* Her gaze slid over him and his companion disdainfully before she deliberately turned away. The blinding smile she awarded Matt gave him pause, before he recovered enough to shoot her an intimate one of his own. Purposefully drawing him out with cleverly worded questions, Alex listened with half an ear and smiled until she thought her face would crack.

A headache was beginning to pound at her temples. Taking a sip of iced water, she dabbed at her lips with her white linen napkin before excusing herself to go to the ladies' room. It was thankfully deserted. Several deep breaths helped calm her down. Damn Ethan and his date anyway. She was welcome to him.

The door opened and closed behind her. The lock clicked into place, echoing loudly in the empty room. She looked up to find Ethan by the door.

A torrent of conflicting emotions flooded her. "Ethan," she greeted him coldly.

His gaze raked over her mockingly as he stepped closer. "Enjoying your date, Alexandra?"

She whipped around to face him. "Enjoying yours?"

One step was all it took to bring him flush against her. With a finger, he traced her glistening lips. "Has he fucked you yet?"

Her breath caught at his blunt words, every muscle stiffening in anger.

He smirked. "I'm guessing he hasn't. What are you doing, Alex? Trying to prove to me that you've moved on?" His voice reverberated with the anger he was making no effort to hide.

Her eyes narrowed. "Are you following me? How did you know I'd be here tonight?"

Broad shoulders moved in a careless shrug. "Emma told me."

She drew in a shaky breath. She'd talked to Emma this morning and casually mentioned she had a date. *Traitor.* Forcing herself to stand still, Alex endured Ethan's hot gaze as it moved slowly to the low neckline of her dress. In an instant, her nipples were hard as pebbles, feeling his gaze like a physical touch. Warm moisture pooled inside her pussy.

His lips curved smugly. "Having fun on your date?"

Alex lifted her chin. "As it happens, I was enjoying myself until you showed up. Go away, Ethan," she added dismissively.

His eyes darkened in anger. "Did you forget the rules, Alex? This is between you and me. We're not allowed to bring anybody else into this."

Cold dread slithered down her spine. "I don't know what you're talking about."

"Liar," he shot back softly. Without warning, he pulled her dress up to her waist and tugged on her flimsy thong. The material ripped easily. In shock, Alex was unable to protest as he pushed her up against the marble sink and knelt in front of her, shouldering her legs apart. In a flash, his stiffened tongue honed in on her slit and marked his territory. She gasped helplessly.

Ethan ate her. Right there in the bathroom of the small, exclusive Le' Duc restaurant. Helpless and powerless to resist, she whimpered and arched. Her body went soft and pliant. The brush of his tongue wasn't gentle—he demanded and received a response. He had no mercy, no qualms about seducing her. He took her clit and bit at it gently. Alex shuddered violently as he fucked her with his tongue, stabbing as deep inside her pussy as he could. With her head tipped back in wanton abandon, she gripped the sink behind her and hung on. A scream formed deep in her throat. He took her so quickly, so erotically that she lost all control. She barely bit back her cries as she came. Pleasure hit her intensely, robbing her of breath, leaving her damp with perspiration. Her body shook with small aftershocks. Her breaths came in harsh pants and were the only sound to be heard in the bathroom for long moments.

His eyes glittered darkly. "Come home with me."

In the silence, the doorknob rattled loudly. They heard a woman's voice through the door. "Hello? Is anybody in there?"

Alex frantically straightened her clothing. "I can't."

He stilled her hands and kissed one palm sensuously. "I don't want to play games with you, Alex. I need you in my bed."

The doorknob rattled again. The woman's irritated voice floated over the locked door. "I'm getting the manager." Her angry footsteps drifted away.

"You have to get out of here," she hissed, completely missing his narrowed gaze. Without saying a word, he turned and left. Shaken, Alex took several deep breaths and splashed cold water on her face. Her galloping pulse showed no signs of slowing down. It was a few moments later before she felt calm enough to walk out of the bathroom. Any second now, Matt was going to come knocking on the door, wondering what the hell was keeping her.

Ethan was right outside the door. Alex threw a glance over to her table and frowned to see Matt wasn't there. Suspicion began to take root in her. "Where is he?"

He shrugged. "It seems he found my date more...ah...willing."

She glared at him. "What do you mean by that?"

The look in his eyes was all too innocent. "They left a few minutes ago. Come on, I'll take you home."

She swatted his hand away. "I can take a cab."

He loomed over her, a big, hot, sexy immovable object. "You can either come with me quietly, or we can make a scene."

Alex tamped down on the insidious arousal weakening her resolve. "Is this where you hit me over the head with your club and drag me off by the hair?" she asked sarcastically.

His jaw tightened grimly. "We can do this either way. Your call, Alex."

Her fists clenched in anger. "You're a bastard. Do you know that?"

In horrified fascination, Alex watched as his control broke. She barely muffled a shriek when he picked her up and threw her over his shoulder. More than a few people threw them curious glances, whispering at the sight. Mortified, Alex shut her eyes to block out the scene of her humiliation.

His car was parked out front. She let out an angry huff as he hustled her into the front seat of the car and quickly fastened the seat belt around her. He didn't miss her furtive glance at the car door.

"You can try, but I'll just drag you back."

Seething with anger, she averted her face and ignored the brief glance he threw her way before pulling out into traffic. Alex took in the passing scenery. "This is not the way home."

He didn't even look at her. "I'm taking you to my home so we can talk."

She scoffed at that. "Talk?"

"Yes, talk," he shot back. "Maybe if you're a good girl, I'll fuck you later and put us both out of our misery."

She was furious at her body's reaction. Why, oh why was this man so irresistible to her? He was like a magnet that continually drew her with his sexual pull. "You wish," she managed to retort with convincing disdain. She turned her face to the window, determined to ignore him.

Apparently content to let her simmer in silence, Ethan drove to his house. He threw the car into park and fairly dragged her through the front door before slamming it shut.

"Sit."

Her chin rose in defiance. She chose the chair farthest away from him and looked at him stonily.

"I've tried to be patient, Alex, but patience doesn't work with you. I'm done playing games." His voice was dangerously quiet.

Feeling at a distinct disadvantage from where she sat, Alex stood up. "I can't believe you would stoop to force." She felt reckless, her anger mixed with arousal. *This wasn't happening, damn it.* Cursing the weakness that attacked her defenses, she stood her ground and faced him. "I know there are plenty of women out there who would be more than glad to take my place."

His brows drew together, his face grim with anger. "This must be my punishment then," he snapped angrily. "Because I want a stubborn, willful woman who is itching for a knockdown, drag-out fight."

She glared at him mulishly.

"Goddammit, there's only one way to communicate with you." He moved so swiftly that she could only gasp in surprise. He hefted her over his shoulder and proceeded up the stairs.

Not again. She kicked him ineffectively. "You better tie me down, because that's the only way you're keeping me here," she declared. Her voice was coldly furious, her face red from hanging upside down directly in line with his tight ass.

"Good idea." He strode into her bedroom and dropped her like a sack of potatoes on his bed. The impact knocked the breath from her and held her immobile for precious moments, long enough for him to fish something out of his drawer. He threw a leg over both of hers to hold her down while he made quick work of her dress. In no time at all, she was naked.

Next, he took both her arms and fastened them above her head with leather handcuffs. Alex struggled furiously, pulling at the restraints. He tied her to the thick columns of the headboard.

"Let me go," she demanded angrily. Her nipples hardened in the cool air of the shadowed bedroom.

"You really think I believe this angry, outraged act?" he asked mockingly. He speared her pussy a heated glance. "Even now, you're getting wet wondering what I'm going to do to you." A grim smile played around his lips. "Perhaps I'll blindfold you. Deprivation of senses heightens pleasure. You won't know what to expect. You'll try to anticipate what I'll do."

She glared at him, chest heaving with every breath.

Holding her gaze, he began to undress. Alex stubbornly averted her eyes. Ethan chuckled softly. "Look at me, Alex."

Still determined to defy him, she closed her eyes. If she was honest with herself, she'd turn and look her fill like she really wanted.

"Look at me, or you won't like the consequences."

Something in his tone made her obey. He was naked, his cock standing at rapt attention, proudly erect and unashamedly aroused. Her mouth went dry. Her eyes were glued to his cock, her thoughts written plainly on her face as she licked suddenly dry lips.

He followed the progress of her tongue. "Later," he said thickly. "For now, I have to teach you a lesson."

"Lesson?" she croaked. Fresh moisture flooded her pussy.

"I am the only one who can give you what you need, Alex." Her body reacted traitorously to his closeness. "Your little act of defiance tonight didn't work. You couldn't take your eyes off me. You were so upset because you were jealous."

"I felt nothing of the sort," she denied huskily, her eyes drawn like a magnet to his cock. *God, I want him in my mouth.*

He rubbed her lips. "Such lies from these lovely lips." He bent low and licked her ear. "You're used to being in control of your emotions and your feelings. You can't control *me*. You can't control your body that's begging to be fucked by me."

He ran a hand over her stomach. Her muscles contracted at his touch. "Let me go, Ethan." Her movements screamed the exact opposite as her legs fell apart to expose her weeping slit.

He chuckled softly as he pressed a soft kiss on her lips. "One week was long enough for me," he whispered. "I missed you so much I couldn't sleep."

He looked at her expectantly.

Her eyes flashed in defiance despite her state of immobility. "All right. I couldn't sleep either. Satisfied?"

"Not by a long shot." He tweaked her nipples gently before pulling one between his lips. The rough rasp of his tongue made her moan helplessly. "I love your breasts. I love their shape, the way they fit in my hands. I love their taste."

Alex tossed her head against the pillow, pulling at the restraints.

He laved her navel with soft licks before moving downwards, his shoulders keeping her thighs apart. "Do you want me to fuck you, Alex?"

With a moan, she pushed her hips closer to him. "Yes," she hissed.

"Then you're going to have to beg me for it." Her eyes widened in disbelief at his words. "I can go on all night without making you come."

"Why are you doing this?" she cried in frustration.

"I want to prove to you that no one else can give you what I can. I'm the only one who can fuck you into a mindless frenzy." His hard, determined tone was at odds with the gentle way he licked all around her pussy. "You can have this every night. All you have to do is admit that I'm the only one you want."

Alex shook her head in mute denial. With a small grin, he settled between her thighs and sought the hidden folds and hollows of her pussy.

"Ohhhh," she moaned helplessly.

Ethan was relentless, determined to make her beg. Alex barely hung on to her sanity as he licked and lapped at her. Her gaze grew unfocused as she looked down at his dark head. Her moans intensified. She was almost there, so close, so—

He stopped.

Alex sobbed in protest. "Ethan, don't do this."

Slowly moving up her sweat-dampened body, he leaned over her, his eyes closed tightly. He held his cock by the base of the shaft and pressed tightly. A moment passed before he breathed deeply.

Her lips parted, her gaze glued to his rampantly erect cock.

Ethan reached over to the nightstand and picked up a thick tube. Her eyes widened as he spread a generous amount of lubricant on his palm and proceeded to coat his cock slowly.

Apprehension warred with desire inside her. Desire won. "Ethan?" Excited anticipation was thick in her voice.

"Don't worry. You'll like this." He put his hands under her knees and pushed up, the position leaving her open and vulnerable. The broad head of his cock nudged the puckered opening of her ass.

Her breath caught in her throat. There was no possible way he was going to fit in there.

"Relax."

"You're killing me," she groaned, trying vainly to shift her hips.

He easily held her firm and steady. "Babe, you'll be reborn after this." His finger went to her pussy and began a steady, mind-destroying massage to her clit.

Pleasure began to work its magic, making her body pulsate deeply, boneless and pliant. His cock pushed through the initial tightness of her rectal muscles before he stopped. "A-Are you…?" she trailed off helplessly. Her eyes rolled to the back of her head at the incredible pleasure/pain that paralyzed her.

He grunted and pushed in slowly, inch by inch, until his balls slapped against her.

Her breath rushed out. "*Oh, God.*"

His eyes locked onto hers. "Feel good?"

Alex was unable to answer, bathed in sweat and panting harshly. She felt every inch of him inside her, initiating muscles unused to such penetration. Unable to help herself, she moved. The slight movement only lodged him deeper. "Ethan, please," she begged. "You have to move. Oh!"

Her thoughts scattered with a touch of his hand. Two fingers slid in her pussy and found her G-spot, starting a maddening come-hither motion. Alex was mindless at the assault on her senses. "Fuck me, please," she begged unashamedly, beyond caring. "*Please.*"

"Feel what your body is telling you. This pussy," his fingers plunged deep into her, "this ass," he punctuated his words with deep thrusts, "is *mine*. Your body recognizes it even if your mind doesn't."

Alex was moaning, out of control.

"You can deny it all you want, Alex. But you want me and nobody else." His words brought her gaze up to his. His jaw was tight, his face dotted with sweat. "Say it."

"Ethan," she gasped.

He stayed unmoving deep inside her. "Say it."

Her eyes softened in surrender. "I'm yours. Yours," she choked out breathlessly, her voice broken. "Fuck me, please."

The deep blue of his eyes flared with satisfaction. He began to fuck her in earnest. Alex writhed on the bed, whimpering helplessly. The sensations that bombarded her drove her insane, her whole being concentrated on the forbidden place where they were joined. He had been ruthless in making her beg. Now that she had surrendered, he fucked her like a crazed man.

She was with him every step of the way, riding every wave and roll of pleasure that slammed through her. At last she screamed and threw her head back, bucking out of control. She tightened rhythmically on his cock, lost in the throes of her orgasm. *I'm dying*, she thought hazily.

Ethan plunged into her one final time before going off the edge. She whimpered, wrapping her legs tightly around his hips. It went on and on. By the time it was over, she was utterly drained of energy.

He untied her wrists, gently rubbing the reddened skin. His eyes met hers before he kissed her tenderly. "I love you Alex."

Shock rendered her speechless.

Tenderly, Ethan pushed a damp tendril of hair away from her cheek. "I know you're wary of commitment. I'm willing to wait and work this out. I just want us to be together." His lips touched hers again and again. "I can't let you go."

Exhausted and sated, Alex blinked away the tears that pricked the corner of her eyes.

"Don't say anything right now," he whispered softly. "Just open yourself to the possibility."

Her heart ached. "Why?"

"Because I love you," was his simple answer. "As long as we're together every day and every night, I'll be happy."

Alex clung to him tightly and buried her face in his neck. She didn't know what she'd done to deserve this chance at true love. Deep in her heart, she knew she loved Ethan as much as he loved her. But old habits died hard. It was difficult to let go of her fear. Ethan believed that they had a future, which was enough for her. With a small sigh, she settled deeper in his arms, her eyes closing as she fell in a deep, dreamless sleep.

Epilogue

Cool, early morning sunlight peeked through the open drapes and into the small breakfast nook. Dressed in one of Ethan's shirts, Alex rubbed her foot against his thigh, enjoying the soft, rasping feel of his body hair against her skin. Mornings like this were her favorite. It was intimate and cozy, filled with simple togetherness. It reminded her of the first morning they'd spent together in this house, one year ago.

One year. *Had it been that long?* She'd moved in and now felt as though she belonged with him. Her eyes shone softly with love as she looked at him. He never failed to take her breath away, even with his hair tousled from sleep and sexy stubble covering his chin. Unable to contain her excitement, she pulled down the newspaper he was reading.

"I sublet my apartment yesterday," she announced.

He grinned. "I know."

She frowned. "You know?"

With a nod, he put the paper aside. "Uh-huh."

Alex leaned back with a pout and a sulky sigh. "I'm not excited anymore."

He gave her an indulgent smile before pulling her onto his lap. "There's not much I don't know about you, sweetheart." He kissed her. "Did I thank you for the wonderful meal you cooked last night?"

She flushed with pleasure. "Only about a hundred times."

His chuckle was muffled against her neck. "I loved it. Everything was perfectly cooked and nothing burned."

With a laugh, she hugged him tightly. "Thank you. I think."

He leaned back. "Don't feel you have to learn how to cook for me, Alex."

"I want to do it for you." Her parted lips touched his. "It gives me pleasure." The kiss lengthened and deepened. Reluctantly, Alex tore her lips away from him before she got completely distracted. She looked at him shyly. "Will you marry me?"

Ethan didn't speak. Alex watched him swallow and looked at him anxiously. He cupped her face in his hands and looked directly into her eyes. "Yes."

Without giving her time to respond, he pulled her to his study. He went behind the desk and took out a velvet box from the drawer. Inside was a beautiful square cut, sparkling diamond, nestled in a thick platinum setting.

Her vision was blurred by the sudden tears in her eyes. "Since when have you had this?"'

The ring slid on her finger, a perfect fit. "I've had it since the day you moved in." He tipped her chin up. "I knew you would come around. I just had to be patient. Even though you agreed to move in with me, you were wary enough to keep your apartment." His voice was filled with gentle rebuke. He held up a hand when she tried to speak. "You needed to have something to fall back on in case things didn't work out between us. Oh, ye of little faith."

She wiped her tears away. "I know. But now I'm ready to make the ultimate commitment." It didn't even hurt anymore to say the word, she realized.

Ethan drew her in for a kiss full of love. "I want to get married soon. We've wasted enough time."

Alex nodded without hesitation. "I talked to my Mom last night."

"And?" he prompted. His hands slid under her shirt, pulling down her thong. His fingers busily delved between her thighs.

Her breathing quickened. "She thinks her latest marriage might work out for good, after all." Her eyes drifted closed, her legs opening obediently for him.

He lifted her in his arms and his cock slid home. It was a perfect fit. Conversation ceased as he started to move smoothly in and out of her pussy. She hugged him tightly, lost in the joy of being with him. She'd been resigned to spending her life alone. She'd never thought she'd find true love. Her lips curved as pleasure began to take over her senses. Life had a way of working out.

Enjoy this excerpt from
Bodyguard

© *Copyright Beverly Havlir, 2005*

All Rights Reserved, Ellora's Cave Publishing, Inc.

Bodyguard

Paige turned away and walked to her bedroom, carefully closing the door behind her. Tears pricked at the corners of her eyes. Muttering under her breath about the unfairness of the world, she toed off her chunky-heeled pumps. She pulled the dress over her head and threw it into the hamper in a fit of rage. Walking to her dresser, she unclasped the single strand of her mother's pearls at her neck and tossed it on the polished top. Next, she attacked the pins holding her hair up and began brushing her hair with merciless tugs, wincing at the pain in her scalp.

To her horror, the brush flew from her hand and skidded across the polished top of the dresser, knocking a bottle of perfume over. The bottle fell over the side and landed on the hardwood floor, crashing into a thousand tiny pieces.

Her bedroom door crashed against the wall. Nick rushed in, his gun in hand. Paige gaped at him, unable to move.

Nick froze. He stared at her, standing amidst broken glass and barely dressed in a low cut silk bra and matching thong. "What the hell happened?" he rasped. He couldn't take his gaze off her.

Paige felt his eyes like a physical caress. The shattered glass lay forgotten. The enticing, sensual scent of the perfume rose between them. She knew she should at least cover herself, but the fire in his eyes rooted her to the spot. Heat seeped through her skin. She felt hot. So hot. She finally summoned the energy to bring an arm up to cover her breasts.

"Don't move," he commanded in a hoarse voice. He flicked the safety on his gun and stuck it in the back of his jeans. He made his way over to her, carefully pushing the broken shards of glass to the side. "Are you hurt?"

She couldn't speak for the huge lump in her throat, so she simply shook her head. There was such heat in his eyes, heat that called an answering firestorm deep inside her. The intensity of it made her knees weak.

"Goddammit Paige, you scared the hell out of me." His hands curved around her waist as he lifted her clear of the sharp glass and deposited her on the other side of the bed.

God, why were his hands so hot on her skin? "It was an accident," she began to explain. Her breath hitched in her throat at the way he was staring at her.

Following the direction of his gaze, Paige flushed even deeper when she saw how the mounds of her too-generous breasts jutted against the cups of the bra. And was that a nipple peeking through the top? She pushed away from him, her eyes darting around for something within reach so she could cover herself.

He stilled her movements. "I can't figure you out." A blunt finger came up and traced her damp lower lip.

Her pulse skittered out of control. She couldn't look away from his dark eyes. "W-what do you mean?"

Nick shifted closer. He was so close that she felt the tremendous heat coming off him in waves. "I can't figure out why a beautiful woman like you would choose to hide under shapeless clothing."

She looked away. His hand gently nudged her chin to turn her face back to him. Her lashes lowered.

He bent his head, his cheek rubbing against hers in a tender, sensuous movement. "I grew up with four sisters. I remember them spending hours and hours trying on new clothes, makeup and hairstyles. They wanted to look beautiful." His finger skimmed over her cheek. "You, however, do the exact opposite. You put your hair in a ponytail, wear eyeglasses that I doubt you really need, and live in jeans and sweatshirts."

She squirmed. Her nipples were tight, painful points pushing against her bra. Unfamiliar warmth began to spread from her lower belly. "Nick," she breathed. What was he doing?

He traced the madly beating pulse at the base of her throat. "Tell me why."

How could she think when he touched her like that? She moaned. At the sound, he bent and brushed his lips against hers. A shudder tore through her as their bodies came into contact. His skin was rough where hers was smooth. She could feel a disturbing length of stiff flesh touching her bare skin.

He plunged his fingers into her hair and tilted her face up. Licking the corner of her lips, he bade her to open her mouth. "Give me your tongue, Paige. Let me taste you."

Her lips parted. Her heartbeat thundered in her ears. She touched her tongue to his, shyly, hesitantly. She jumped when a sound rumbled from his lips. "Nick?"

"Do it again," he ordered gruffly.

"This?" she asked, touching her tongue to his. He emitted a sound between a groan and a growl before he took over and pushed inside her mouth.

She moaned. Her limbs felt heavy and weightless. His hands splayed on her back, pulling her closer and keeping her there. Her senses whirled. Their lips parted and clung together again and again. She was breathing hard when he eventually let her up for air.

Enjoy this excerpt from
Pleasure Planet

© *Copyright Claire Thompson, Beverly Havlir, 2005*

All Rights Reserved, Ellora's Cave Publishing, Inc.

EROS

She was trembling, trying to catch her breath. Ronan pulled her to him, locking her in his embrace. He whispered in her ear, "Aria. Aria. Calm yourself. You're shivering. All you need to do is relax and to obey me. I won't demand anything of you that you don't already want — don't already crave. Sometimes our fantasies aren't clear, even to ourselves. I'll help you to unlock them. You can trust me, my love. I exist solely for you."

Slowly her heart stopped its insistent hammering against her ribs. Her breathing eased as the strong man held her in his arms. She leaned her head against his shoulder and realized he smelled nice.

That's right, she reminded herself, *he exists solely for me!* This was her week! She'd paid an extraordinary sum for the peculiar adventure now facing her. The reputation of the place was stellar. The Erosians must know what they were doing. This man wasn't her kidnapper, he was really *her* sex slave as it was her money that had purchased this lark. He could pretend to be her lord and master all he liked. She knew the real situation.

And if damsel in distress was the fantasy they were going to play, well, why not? It would be fun! Ronan's hands, which had been gripping her bare shoulders, dropped now to her ass. He cupped the round globes and squeezed.

"Think what you like, Aria. It may only be a week but it's going to be much more than a game, I assure you. Yes, you bought the time and the experience, but you cannot just turn it off at your whim. Now you have to play by the rules — my rules.

"I'm going to give you pleasure you've never experienced before. I promise you that. I know you're used to getting exactly what you want, exactly when you want it. That may not be the case this week. I'm going to test you. And as with any test worth its merit, there will be rewards as well as punishments. Real punishments, not playacting. I'm going to take you beyond the limits you've set with your conscious mind. Do you understand what I'm saying?"

Aria surveyed the handsome man before her. This lovely specimen of male human perfection was giving her the "script" for their luscious little game. He was laying out the rules by which he would pretend to be her lord and master. Slowly she nodded, smiling slightly.

TRISTAN'S WOMAN

The heavy beat of drums filled the air and gradually rose to a resounding crescendo. Every male in the lounge, human and alien, sat forward in eagerness, all eyes glued to the stage. Driven by an intense curiosity that he didn't question, Tristan edged closer to the platform. The music switched to a stirring, sensual rhythm. A lone spotlight focused on the center of the platform. The curtains twitched then slowly parted.

A smooth, shapely leg appeared. A strange fluttering sensation started somewhere in Tristan's chest. The hairs on the back of his neck stood on end. A voluptuous woman draped in thin veils swayed into view, dressed in sheer, loose pants and a top that barely contained her generous breasts. She undulated onto the stage, her smooth belly dipping and rippling with every sensuous movement.

Tristan's cock hardened instantly. His breath stuck somewhere between his lungs and his throat. His computer monitor flashed, indicating a drastic change in his body temperature. He inhaled deeply, unable to take his eyes off the woman dancing on stage.

Long, golden-blonde hair fell down her back in glorious, tousled waves. Her lowered gaze hid the color of her eyes, the long lashes creating half-moon shadows on her cheeks. He was struck by the fullness of her rosebud lips and her small, perfect nose. The graceful arch of her neck invited a man's touch. As she swayed and turned, her breasts were pulled taut by her outstretched arms, their heavy weight straining the thin material of her top.

Blood rushed to his cock, lengthening it to its full size. His system showed a marked increase in his pulse rate as she executed a graceful turn, the veils falling around her in a filmy cloud. Tristan stood as close as he could to the stage, unable to take his eyes off her. He was mesmerized by the sexy sway of her hips. Every shake of her soft body drew his eyes to her womanly hips and to the plump curves of her buttocks. She was lushly formed, generously shaped, perfect for fucking.

Before the night was over, he was going to have her.

Why an electronic book?

We live in the Information Age—an exciting time in the history of human civilization in which technology rules supreme and continues to progress in leaps and bounds every minute of every hour of every day. For a multitude of reasons, more and more avid literary fans are opting to purchase e-books instead of paperbacks. The question to those not yet initiated to the world of electronic reading is simply: *why?*

1. *Price.* An electronic title at Ellora's Cave Publishing and Cerridwen Press runs anywhere from 40-75% less than the cover price of the exact same title in paperback format. Why? Cold mathematics. It is less expensive to publish an e-book than it is to publish a paperback, so the savings are passed along to the consumer.

2. *Space.* Running out of room to house your paperback books? That is one worry you will never have with electronic novels. For a low one-time cost, you can purchase a handheld computer designed specifically for e-reading purposes. Many e-readers are larger than the average handheld, giving you plenty of screen room. Better yet, hundreds of titles can be stored within your new library—a single microchip. (Please note that Ellora's Cave and Cerridwen Press does not endorse any specific brands. You can check our website at www.ellorascave.com or

www.cerridwenpress.com for customer recommendations we make available to new consumers.)

3. *Mobility*. Because your new library now consists of only a microchip, your entire cache of books can be taken with you wherever you go.
4. *Personal preferences are accounted for*. Are the words you are currently reading too small? Too large? Too…**ANNOYING**? Paperback books cannot be modified according to personal preferences, but e-books can.
5. *Instant gratification*. Is it the middle of the night and all the bookstores are closed? Are you tired of waiting days—sometimes weeks—for online and offline bookstores to ship the novels you bought? Ellora's Cave Publishing sells instantaneous downloads 24 hours a day, 7 days a week, 365 days a year. Our e-book delivery system is 100% automated, meaning your order is filled as soon as you pay for it.

Those are a few of the top reasons why electronic novels are displacing paperbacks for many an avid reader. As always, Ellora's Cave and Cerridwen Press welcomes your questions and comments. We invite you to email us at service@ellorascave.com, service@cerridwenpress.com or write to us directly at: 1056 Home Ave. Akron OH 44310-3502.

The
☥ Ellora's Cave ☥
Library

Stay up to date with Ellora's Cave Titles in
Print with our Quarterly Catalog.

To recieve a catalog,
send an email with your name
and mailing address to:

CATALOG@ELLORASCAVE.COM

or send a letter or postcard
with your mailing address to:

Catalog Request
c/o Ellora's Cave Publishing, Inc.
1056 Home Avenue
Akron, Ohio 44310-3502

Ellora's Cavemen
Legendary Tails

Try an e-book for your immediate reading pleasure or order these titles in print from

www.EllorasCave.com

COMING TO A BOOKSTORE NEAR YOU!

ELLORA'S CAVE

Bestselling Authors Tour

UPDATES AVAILABLE AT
WWW.ELLORASCAVE.COM

Cerridwen, the Celtic Goddess of wisdom, was the muse who brought inspiration to storytellers and those in the creative arts. Cerridwen Press encompasses the best and most innovative stories in all genres of today's fiction. Visit our site and discover the newest titles by talented authors who still get inspired - much like the ancient storytellers did, once upon a time.

Cerridwen Press
www.cerridwenpress.com

*Discover for yourself why readers can't get enough of the multiple award-winning publisher
Ellora's Cave.
Whether you prefer e-books or paperbacks, be sure to visit EC on the web at
www.ellorascave.com
for an erotic reading experience that will leave you breathless.*